The Trials
Secrets, Spells and Tales

By: Liz Rau

Though the Salem Witch Trials were a very real historical event, this book is a work of fiction. Any references to this period of time are purely used for creative purposes. Any events, names, characters, things, situations or places are one of two things: created from pure imagination or used fictitiously; and any parallels otherwise are coincidental and unintended. And as far the author is aware, there are no mentions of gypsies included in any reference on any history book page in relation to events included in this book.

Printed by CreateSpace, An Amazon.com Company

Available on Kindle and other online stores

CreateSpace ISBN-13: 978-1535330664
CreateSpace ISBN-10: 153533066X

Edited by: Liz Rau & Katie Rau

Cover Design: Mathew Jennings

Information: LizRauInfo@gmail.com

I dedicate this book to the dreamers of the world.

Never give up.

TABLE OF CONTENTS

"There are some things I know for certain: always throw spilt salt over your left shoulder, keep rosemary by your garden gate, plant lavender for luck, and fall in love whenever you can."

(From the film *Practical Magic*)

Salem, Massachusetts is known for witchcraft and sorcery, and quite a storied past, but I only know it for the town that stole my heart. It's not that I, Sarah Elizabelle Felix, disbelieved in witchcraft, I had just never experienced it for myself and I've always found it hard to deny something I've never tried or seen firsthand. It's like people who do not believe in God, but yet they've never tried praying.

Perhaps I'm more open-minded to the idea of a mystical world because I'm from a town only known for being small and with no distractions to entertain me, I never denied my imagination to create or a good daydream to consume me. Life before Salem was not much lived and unequivocally dull. Salem brought excitement into my days. Where else on Earth was there a place with such a heavy magical past, and so rich in culture, history and art?

Yet, I do identify with always being different and never fitting into the scene of the narrative. Something... has always felt a bit out of reach from my well-manicured grasp.

After Fate threw me some devastating curveballs at the tender age of twenty, I wandered through life searching for my soul, my place, my meaning to

2

this life.

At the less-tender age of twenty-five, a journey to Boston turned into an afternoon of driving north on a whim - a hunch - a magnetic pull - until I saw signs for Salem Commons and turned towards the tiny town with a huge history. A history, it seems, many still whisper about.

The town looks like the back lot of a studio in Burbank, California. Seriously, this is what Salem actually looks like. It's stunningly picturesque. The morning mist off the sea brings the most mystical pink light into the harbor that enchants me.

It's hard to explain, but as I toured around the Salem Commons that afternoon in early

September, I felt at home. It was
as if something just clicked into
my heart and my soul started to
breathe for the very first time.

Are you aware that witches
sometimes have an animal, also
known as a familiar? Most would
say the animal chooses the person,
but well, I would have to say
Salem is my familiar and it chose
me. It was just a mere two weeks
later that I was living here, in my
two-bedroom condo, sitting on the
balcony with my black fur-ball-of-
a-cat Hanks, sipping on my
homemade soy latte and watching
the boats leave the harbor that
day. With so many different sized
vessels and ships, only one had
ever captured my attention. And
on this particular morning, that

ship, a three-masted black schooner with a gold trim, was limping back into port.

I only bring any of these things up because it was this day, sitting on my balcony sipping a latte that my story really began. All I ask, as you read these pages, is that you allow yourself to breathe and believe, and above all, just let life be.

That's when the magic happens.

Sarah Elizabelle Felix

CHAPTER ONE

Harry stood at the bow of The Craft and let out a deep sigh of despair as he watched the Salem coastline grow closer that morning. His first mate Callen shot him a sideways glance, the sigh taunting him to make a jab at Harry's expense. Harry chose to ignore the sarcastic look and kept his gaze straight. He knew what it was about. Harry hated going home - if he could even call it that. The Craft was his home and she wouldn't be sailing again anytime soon. Cold weather was about to set in and she was not a ship for winter floats in the chilly Atlantic. She'd barely come through that storm last night in one piece and it was going to take Harry the rest of the fall season before the repairs were done.

Callen had called Harry's callous and gruff mood days ago, telling the whole crew not to piss him off the day they docked, unless of course, they didn't want their jobs again come spring. "That ol' Irish temper ya know," he had said. "It can be a fiercer lashing than a fist."

Irish temper. Ha, what a laugh, Harry thought. Harry Ellison was a direct descendent of a Puritan Englishman named John Porter, Jr. The Porter family was notoriously associated to Salem from the fact they were directly linked to the infamous blemish on the town's history. A blemish that marked the Porter family heritage as well.

Now, over three hundred years later, Harry still felt the curse that had befallen the Porter family from those dangerous times where malicious gossip, a struggle for power, and a deep-rooted fear in the Devil himself eventually destroyed one of the first major ports for the East Indian Trade.

The reasons for the The Trials have become misconstrued and ill-famed over the centuries with many forgetting what ignited the witch hunt. It all originally began with two households: the Putnam and the Porter families. The men of these families were sworn enemies with a long-standing rivalry, and it was a hateful battle for dominant control of the land and political leadership. It was a battle for power, Man's greatest weakness.

Ultimately, this struggle for power is what fueled The Trials, though that knowledge seemed all but forgotten these days. The brutality came to a head when the Porter men sabotaged fields harvested by the Putnam family, depleting the ability to maintain their crops that season. After that, the vicious war placed many in the village at odds, forcing them to choose a side.

The Putnam family, on the front of bringing morale to the community, brought the good and honorable Reverend Samuel Parris to the community. As a man of God and peace, surely calmness would blanket the village with his presence. Hope didn't remain long, however, as it was in the Reverend's home where the accusations of witchcraft and the accompanying afflictions first came to light. And though most people know the story of The Trials from there, very few have ever known of the black curse that was laid at the door of the Porter and Putnam families.

The Parris household had been home to a slave named Tituba and it was one of the Parris daughters who'd accused her of black arts and sorcery. Harry always assumed growing up and hearing these stories that Tituba was probably innocent and simply in the wrong place at the wrong time. He'd assumed she'd been an easy target. Harry's assumption couldn't have been further from the truth.

See, though Tituba was known to be a bit of a fortune-teller for the villagers in those days, it was later discovered that she was indeed the only real witch ever accused. She had even admitted those truths to the law during The Trials and claimed she only used occult knowledge to ward away evil. Somehow, Tituba was the only witch not executed during those times and the witch was banished back to her homeland.

Before Tituba left, however, she darkly cursed those who paved the path of her destruction. She hexed the families who lit the match that burned the fueled accusations. For eternity, the two instigating families would not know a home until their burden was buried and a bond was born. She was ruthless in the spell and every generation ultimately paid their dues.

The problem now was that Harry is the last known descendent of either family. Both of the families lost their respective prosperity and wealth, and neither had ever gained it back. Harry had somehow managed to accrue his own small fortune after years of hard work, but only time would tell if his luck would remain.

Strange accidents and deaths occurred on both sides of the ancestral trees throughout the many years and Harry knew those events had indeed been due to the curse, whether it was real or not. All a person had to do was believe and the destruction would be set in motion. As a child, Harry hadn't believed in these fairytales his grandfather would repeatedly refer to as sound reasoning, but as an adult, he now knew better.

Harry was acutely aware that after three hundred and twenty-four years, nothing had really changed. Hearsay and gossip still ruled the community, verily so. All one had to do was look at a news broadcast to see that all types of societies still appeared violently skeptical of any person whose beliefs and values differed from that of their own. He often wondered when history would begin to teach the present generations a new path of resolutions.

The whispers and judgment was why Harry's great-grandfather decided to change the family's last name to Ellison years ago. Hardly anybody in Salem could recall that Harry – Harold Tucker Ellison – was in fact, a Porter descendent.

The squawk of a seagull landing on the railing jarred Harry back to reality, causing him to recall Callen's Irish temper comment and he rolled his eyes again. It was the hair color that had people assuming he was of Irish descent. His scalp was thickly covered with flame colored ginger bristles, as was his five o'clock shadow of whiskers that were beginning to form a beard. He was grateful though, that people mistook him for Irish because he did indeed have a temper each time he made port in Salem's harbor. And as Callen liked to point out, it showed up just like clockwork.

Harry was unsure of how long he had actually been standing there, with his white-knuckle grasp on the railing, stewing about the fact he wouldn't be able to leave Salem again for a while, but his trance broke when he heard Callen's sharp intake of breath. He quizzically peered at him and then followed Callen's gaze to the shore, and his heart almost stopped when he found the subject of fascination, and his ocean-blue eyes widened in awe.

There on a balcony of a nearby residence, in the light of the pink-toned sunrise, stood a beautiful woman with wildly long raven hair. Harry was fairly sure there was no breeze, the surrounding trees weren't moving at all, yet her hair was blowing around her as if she was the one standing at the bow of a ship making port. And she was looking at them. The second that their eyes met Harry felt a connection. His arms quickly flushed with goose flesh and his mouth went dry, as though he had attempted to flirt and failed miserably – not that Harry experienced that scenario very often. And within him, somewhere deep and untouched, he felt a humming. *Why do I feel like I know her?*

He blinked and in a moment's time, the balcony was empty. *Had she even been there?* Harry wasn't entirely sure she was real to begin with. But then again, it wasn't likely possible for him and Callen to have the same hallucination, even in a town full of witches. Was it?

CHAPTER TWO

Sarah sat in the Salem Commons with her trusty sketchpad drawing the schooner she had been studying from her balcony earlier that morning. For a week now her psyche had been dreaming of such a ship and she had been repeatedly depicting its shapes, its sails and its fluidity. This morning had presented her something else to portray with her pencil outlines. Besides two of the three masts being split and some chunks missing from the port side, there had been a man at the bow. Technically there had been two men, but only the one had resonated with her.

As she closed her eyes she could still see his tall strong figure gripping the railing, his blazing hair outlined by the misty pink sunrise and she had sworn, even though she hadn't been close enough to tell, that his eyes were the same color as the sea. She wondered if they perhaps changed with the color of the current.

When a small black bird landed on her black laced-up boot, her eyes popped up, and she was shocked to see the mysterious stranger strolling into view. Without hesitation, she hopped off the bench, with her sketchpad and purse in tow, ducked around a tree and into a bookshop named Candlesticks. *What was that?* She curiously wondered at her actions. Why the sudden fear that he may see her? Or was it that her art project would be discovered? *Or discover my admiration of his stormy eyes.*

Sure he hadn't seen her, she stuffed the sketches

into her bag and moved away from the window. She'd wanted to pick up a book on the history of Salem anyway, so how coincidental this shop had been right there. *Now seems to be as good as a time as any*, she thought.

The shop was cute and had a comfort-factor about it, as though one was more than welcome to curl up with a coffee and dream for a while. It made Sarah smile as she went in search of historical knowledge, witchy or not. Most of what she came across in the 'About the Town' section seemed to be based on The Trials. There were only four books that appeared to be comprehensive histories of Salem and she automatically put two back since they didn't have any pictures. She had to see images; she had always been a very visual person. It was the only way she seemed to retain information – when she could carry the picture in her mind.

In fact, that's how Sarah had known she was adopted. When she was a mere seven-years-old, sitting in her mom's lap, perusing through family photo albums when she stopped to tell her mother that she knew she wasn't her daughter by blood, but that was the way it was supposed to be. Then Sarah simply returned her focus to the photos, as if no major emotional bomb was dropped with her statement, and her adoption just a simply matter-of-fact detail, like her height or hair color. Now, most kids at age seven are only interested in knowing what types of cartoons they could watch or how many cookies they could have before bedtime. Sarah hadn't been concerned with those things. She was a very intellectual child and could never lie, not even one little fib. And she always had this guttural instinct about her. For as long as Sarah could remember, she seemed to somehow always know an answer before a question was asked. Except when the question was her own, of course. Sarah's path had never been clear in her mind.

When her mother had asked how she knew about the adoption, Sarah first stated she 'just did'. When her mom gaped back at her, she continued to tell her that it was simply scientific reasoning; she had to be adopted. Not one other person in her family had black wavy hair and big blue eyes. In fact, both her parents and her grandparents had stick straight blonde hair and small green eyes. To an overly curious and inquisitive child like Sarah the facts had merely been obvious. Even more, though, Sarah had just been able to see the truth. It was as though she had a mind's eye, and it saw what Sarah felt she knew within... somehow. *But I always recognized their love for me,* Sarah thought. *That had never been a question.*

Kids she went to school with hadn't much cared for her though, and they never hid their distaste either. Because of her long, and often unruly black mane, and pale porcelain skin, the other children had called her a witch. She now thought that was pretty ironic since she was living in what was basically deemed Witchville, USA. The nickname lasted all the way through elementary school and but by the time she had made it to junior high, it had seemingly been forgotten. Sarah never forgot it though. It had clung to her like a coat of armor.

In fact, Sarah actually became quite popular by the time high school arrived. She joined nearly every club or group possible, and even won prom princess during her junior year. She knew that, even then, her popularity was solely based on the same thing that had haunted her youth, the very same reason kids had termed her a witch for years: her looks. Black hair and sapphire-hued eyes made for quite the exotic outer shell.

After she left high school, she attended a college out-of-state and retained none of her relationships from her childhood. After all, why would she? They hadn't ever really known her, so why bother keeping those people around as friends? Sarah certainly hadn't expected them to stay in touch and those expectations had not let her down. In so many ways, high school had never seemed real to her - because she never really belonged.

Her sophomore year of college was when her life took a downward spiral. Both of Sarah's parents and her only living grandparents died in plane crash. The guilt was a hump she never managed to climb over. Her family had been on their way to see her, and by some freak accident with the landing gear, the plane crashed on the runway and killed her four only remaining relatives. Nobody else on the plane died on that horrific day – just her family. The memory of telling her family about the weariness of them flying that particular morning still overwhelmed her. She'd had a terrible pit in her gut and warned her family not to fly. Saying how much they wanted to see her, they boarded the Charleston-bound flight anyways. Her heart still felt stained.

In spite of Sarah's grief she finished college - because her parents would've wanted her to - and moved back home to her parent's house in Missouri. She got a job, because that's what you were supposed to do after college, but she hadn't much cared for her career. It'd never felt satisfying or challenging. The motions she put herself through everyday left her feeling numb. Always numb.

Her world was rocked once again when she turned twenty-five and discovered she was to inherit all of her grandparents estate, which made her rich enough to buy all of Salem if she felt ever-so inclined. After laying black magic roses on their tombs, she said goodbye to her beloved family and left Missouri altogether in search of fulfillment. Something had been missing in her life and she was determined to discover what it was.

Sarah traveled in a spirit of wanderlust, alone except for her cat Hanks. The precocious black cat was her only friend and had been with her since college. She soon discovered that nowhere in the world were people compliant to seeing a cat on a leash, but Hanks wasn't the typical cat she supposed. Hanks often voiced his opinions and Sarah would swear to it that he answered her questions. He also seemed to be in agreement with Sarah's search for wander and was quite the comfortable companion.

And for the first time in her life, Sarah Elizabelle Felix realized there wasn't any reason not to find out where she had come from. What was her history? Her story?

After finding her adoption papers, she went to Boston as the papers indicated the agency her parents used was there. A quick Google search gave her the current address. The only problem was, when she found the place, it had burnt down - walls and all - two days earlier. All the records, the files, the answers, had gone up in smoke and flames with it. *Who still keeps the dinosaur-old paper filing systems anyway? Talk about ancient*, she thought. For the second time in five years she felt cursed.

Then a breeze swirled around her, dandelions dancing in the air, and she looked up to see a sign for Salem Tours – A Bewitching Hour. That was the day she'd spontaneously drove to Salem and started her life over.

Sarah sighed as she picked herself up off the floor, unsure of the moment she'd even made herself so comfortable. Having completely zoned out and not bothering to look at either book, she groaned. *Oh well, I'll just buy both. It's not like I can't afford it now.* She took them up to the owner who doubled as a cashier and smiled.

"Both please," she said as she set them on the counter.

"Sure thing sweetie." The owner, with her blonde bouncy curls, was dressed in black, head-to-toe, except for her fingernails. There were indigo blue. "Are you a tourist?"

"No... I just moved into town actually."

The voluminous curly-haired blonde raised an eyebrow. "Are you a witch?"

Having already gotten this question several times, Sarah just laughed. "No, not that I know of. Are you?"

The petite owner broke into a smile. "Well duh," she smiled prettily. "I'm a white witch."

Somehow her answer didn't faze Sarah. "And that means?"

"It means I harm none, even though they deserve it sometimes, and I am considered a healer. Also I see truth in people or their actions. I'm not Wiccan, however, I don't belong to a coven." She smiled again and Sarah realized how young she must be, probably the same age as herself. "My name is Kirsten." She seemed friendly enough as her hand shot out between them.

Sarah took her hand to shake it but Kirsten gasped, pulling away.

"You aren't new here." Her voice had lowered in curiosity.

"Yes, yes I am. I just moved here from Missouri."

"That's not what I meant. Here, hold on a sec." Kirsten left and Sarah could hear her open a drawer. "Okay," she said, returning and clutching a deck of cards in her hand, "pick one".

Sarah was interested enough to stay and find out what Kirsten meant, so she chose the second card and turned it over. *Oh, Tarot Cards.* She drew Death. *Holy crap.*

As if she read her mind, Kirsten reassured her. "No, it doesn't mean you are going to die. Death represents the beginning of a new life and that your old one has served it's purpose. You are about to go through major changes, some abrupt and some due to past events."

"Oh, well, I did come here to start over."

"Draw one more."

Judgment.

"It means awakening or rebirth."

"Of what?"

"I feel you'll figure it out. Hey, is that your car outside?"

"Yeah it is." Sarah didn't bother to look up; she was still looking at Death and Judgment.

"And is Harry a friend of yours or is he playing Peeping Tom to your Audi?"

"Who?" That jarred her and she looked up to see a familiar ginger-headed daydream drooling over her car. *Damn, he's almost too good looking up close.*

"Yes, yes he is," Kirsten winked. "You should see his butt."

Sarah really had to find a way to keep her thoughts to herself.

CHAPTER THREE

Harry had never been so sore from a sail before but he refused to go home. He just couldn't, not yet. His mood had lifted, though somewhat unexpectedly, after seeing *her* on the balcony. He couldn't figure it out. *Why had he noticed her?* Tons of people had been on the docks that morning, even though it had been early, and not one of them had his caught his attention, not one other person at all. Harry really wanted to blame his distraction on Callen but honestly, he was glad he saw the mysterious stranger, and he wanted to see the raven haired beauty again. It was the strangest sensation, but Harry almost felt like they *had* to meet.

Did he feel that? *What the Hell is wrong with me? Ugh I just need some caffeine.* He had stupidly decided to walk in from the docks to the Commons and only just realized what an unmitigated ass he had been when turning down a perfectly good ride from a member of his crew. He was now going to be even sorer, and in a much more blackened mood by the time he did decide to make his way home. *Maybe I should just go to The Brew and get a stiff scotch instead.*

He started to change his course when he saw a flash of raven hair go behind the tree. He moved so he could see who it was but she was gone. Did he really see her? Or is he just wanting to? Was he losing his mind? *Nope, I should definitely stick to coffee.*

The Broom & Cup was maybe his favorite little coffee shop in all of Massachusetts. Sure, during October it wasn't so great because of the tourist surge throughout the town, but his friend Mathew owned it and it was like another home-away-from-home. Harry needed as many of those as feasibly possible. And every once in awhile he even helped his buddy out of an overflow jam. Harry thought he had pretty great barista and cheesecake-serving skills, and was fairly confident though skills were earning rave reviews online.

All the delectable goods were homemade and the seating was designed of mismatched couches and chairs that synchronized with mismatched cups and saucers. Every piece went together in the same way that Picasso paintings makes sense. As he stepped through the door of the tiny shop, he heard the familiar bell-chime welcoming him home.

"Hey man, didn't know you were back yet." Mat practically flew past him like a witch on her broomstick, muffins in hand.

Mat's fly-by greeting clued him into the frantic business of the shop, so Harry stepped directly behind the bar and grabbed the pot of black coffee and the pot of hot water for tea. "Yeah, just got in this morning. Be right back." He stepped back around the bar and danced his way through the tables, refilling teacups and mugs as he went. His darkened haze seemed to fade away as the patron's smiles and thank you's soothed his flaming ruffled feathers.

Mat chuckled, "thanks man. Good to see you're still in one piece."

Harry returned the empty pots and started a new brew for the coffee. "Just barely, The Craft really got knocked about last night, two masts are broken."

"Just let me know when you need help and I'll meet you on deck, cappy."

Harry gave him a pointed look at the use of the disturbing nickname and surveyed the crowded coffee shop. "I think you have all you can handle here Mat. How's Ally doing?"

"She's four months pregnant and hormonal. Everything she bakes now tastes like poison. It's me you need to be worried about mate."

Harry raised an eyebrow.

"Blissfully, barely surviving. And slightly starving."

Harry burst out laughing. "You know, I think you're getting gray hair too."

Mat lifted up a giant spoon to look at his reflection. "Really? I guess I should be glad I made it to thirty-two. At least I'm not balding."

Harry shook his head; glad he wasn't as into his own looks. He walked around and sat at a stool in front of Mat. "Sir, I'd like a triple latte."

Mat put down the spoon and looked around him. "What? Couldn't just make your own while you were behind the counter, which is against the rules of the sign," he pointed up to an adjacent sign that stated just that, "As you re-filled and re-brewed the regular stuff? Not that I'm ungrateful," he quickly added in what breath.

"I'm still a paying customer."

"You're a sarcastic ass is what you are."

Harry knew that was true. He also knew that Mat would put up with his moods and mock humor, which is exactly why he did it. He glanced out the window took notice of a shiny black convertible, all but glinting in the sunlight, parked on the opposite side of the Commons. "Mat, do you know whose car that is?"

Mat shook his head and set down Harry's coffee order. "Saw it for the first time in town last week."

Harry set a bill down on the counter and stood up. "Thanks pal. See you tomorrow?"

"Sure thing."

Harry stepped out of the shop and crossed the square. As he got closer, his suspicions were confirmed. The black car wasn't just any car. No, it was an Audi R8 Spyder, convertible, fully loaded, and begging to be raced up the Massachusetts coastline. More interestingly to Harry, it had red interior. It was exactly like his cabin on The Craft. Two gold bangles wrapped around the gearshift to accent the interior. He was impressed; this car was slick.

"If you're going to steal it, just get on with it already."

Gob smacked, again for the second time that day, Harry's mouth went dry when he looked up. *It's her. I didn't imagine it.* Now that Harry was much closer he got a good, appreciative, study of her. She was breathtaking with her azure-jewel colored eyes and raven hair that was wavy and rowdy, yet perfect. She was slim but curvy and maybe 5'5 or 5'6, but it was hard to tell with the tall boots she was wearing on her slim legs that were, again, perfection. He couldn't really see anything else she was wearing because he was once more entranced by her face. Her delicate high cheekbones were blushed with a light pink rose color, her small button nose was almost aristocratic and her lips were as red as an apple. *Was he dribbling drool?*

"You just dropped your latte into my car."

Trance broke.

"Shit!" Harry looked down, she was right. He had just potentially ruined her driver's seat.

"No, latte." She mockingly double-pointed into the car interior.

Sarcasm? "I am so sorry. Here-" Harry removed his sweatshirt to dab the mess, "let me clean it up."

She strolled up to the other side of the car with Kirsten in tow. Harry hadn't even realized Kirsten was there until just now. That fact the both women became so visibly amused extremely irritated him, and mentally Harry kicked himself.

"Seriously, it's okay. No, don't bother; I'll just have my car cleaned. It's fine." Maybe Harry was imagining it, but he thought she looked a bit flushed.

"At least let me pay for it."

"That's not necessary, I was going to have it cleaned at some point this week anyways."

As she smiled Harry was acutely aware that his whole body went numb. *How come I'm extremely embarrassed and she thinks it's humorous? No chance of a date now*, he thought. *Date? Whoa. Who am I right now?* He seemed to sober with realization of his thoughts and found that his blood was circulating again.

"Harry," Kirsten said, "we were just about to go get a latte ourselves. Would you like for us to get another one for you?" She glanced down at the wet red interior of the Audi, "and we'll just give this some time to dry."

Both Harry and the beautiful blue-eyed stranger looked questioningly at her. Obviously they hadn't been about to get coffee. Kirsten just gave him a slight nod of encouragement and his mind shifted into her view.

"I think I'll just go with you, if you don't mind Miss...?" He looked questionably at the woman who had distracted him so much he had dropped his java.

"Just call me Sarah."

And then she smiled once more at Harry and he realized he was a bit of a goner - even if he didn't want to be.

CHAPTER FOUR

Sarah had been nervous from the second she saw him through the Candlesticks storefront window. Suddenly it seemed time had stood still for a moment, maybe two, and then she felt flutters throughout her entire core being. This time, she hadn't wanted to scamper away and even thought she had been funny when she accused him of wanting to steal her car.

Oddly, she couldn't bring herself to look him in the eyes for longer than a few seconds. It was weird – there was in intense sensation of a strong mesmeric draw to this man - it almost hurt to shift her gaze anywhere but his stormy eyes. And she didn't think he made the scene any more composed, seeing as how he just stood there gawking at her. The whole thing left her feeling utterly uncomfortable.

Harry dropping his coffee is what broke the ice, and the magnetic tether she was becoming consumed with. And then he had taken off his sweatshirt, revealing a black undershirt, a sun-kissed tan, and nicely chiseled arms that bode well to the story underneath the shirt. Sarah was glad he wasn't gawking at her still because she had definitely been blushing throughout the interaction. *And doing a little gawking myself*, she realized. The man was downright hot at what had to be at least 6'2, broad shouldered, and even though he was a ginger by hair color, there wasn't one freckle in sight. Sarah thought she detected a gentle giant under his rugged appearance too.

To admit she was more than just a bit startled when Kirsten suggested they were already on their way to get coffee was an understatement. It was an untruth and she didn't think she covered her surprised reaction quickly enough. Sarah had never felt comfortable with fibs, yet, coffee with new friends seemed like a wise choice. Sarah would just have to wait until later to figure out what Kirsten had meant about not being new to Salem. The tarot card readings had been very impressive though. *Nail on the head*, she thought.

As Sarah entered The Broom & Cup with them she knew she was crushing on the nook the moment she stepped inside. Nothing matched but yet, it did. It was a little like eclectic orderly chaos. *Like life*, she thought. As the three of them walked straight to the bar, she found she was forcing herself to ignore the skin-tingling sensation caused by people staring at her. They, too, probably thought she was a witch. She assumed it was because of the black hair and in Salem; every other storefront pertained to a magical necessity of some type.

She was about to place an order for herself when Kirsten interjected and ordered for all three of them. She was accurate with her requests and even got the soymilk correct on her latte, which nearly shook Sarah's calm resolve. *How does she do that?* Although supremely quirky, she liked Kirsten, and had a good feeling about her.

"Harry, where'd your shirt go?" The guy behind the bar placed their coffees on the bar and looked quizzically at Harry.

"I, er, spilled my coffee Mat. That's why I'm here for another."

"He's such a klutz, that fool," the jolly-faced man said to Sarah. "I'm Mat."

"Sarah. It's nice to meet you Mat." She shook his hand. Mat was really *very* handsome too. His dark blond hair curled up, just at the ends, and he had a bit of scruff on his chin and neck that was a little red-tinted, and green eyes that were slightly lighter than an emerald. And he was tall, very tall, and looked to be about the same age as Harry. *What's in the water in Salem?*

Mat leaned forward with a boyish grin on his face, completely relaxing Sarah, and she found herself smiling back at him. "So Harry spilled his coffee huh? Were you there? Was it really wicked embarrassing? Please say yes!" The humor in his eyes was contagious and it was obvious he was trying hard not to laugh.

Sarah could tell Harry's mood was beginning to bristle though and thought better of joining Mat's game, "I'll tell you about it some other time," she winked.

"Deal. Sit anywhere you like." He gestured to his shop, which was when she realized how popular it must be – there were barely any open seats! Only one space was large enough to accommodate room for all three of them. Towards the front of the shop by a large storefront window sat a green and white polka dotted circular couch with a large brown trunk serving as a coffee table. The trio sat with Kirsten placing her small frame in between them.

"So," Harry turned to her, "where are you from?"

"What makes you think I'm not from around here?

"Because I was born and raised in Salem. I know everybody."

"Missouri."

"What?"

"Missouri. I'm from Missouri."

"You're a long way from home, aren't you?"

"No she's not," Kirsten interrupted their dull chatter. "She just moved here."

"Why?" Harry took a sip of his latte.

"Why not?"

"People don't really move to Salem. Unless, of course, it's for yet another tourist shop, and you don't strike me as that sort. Otherwise, people typically prefer Boston."

Sarah looked at Kirsten. *I don't want to talk about it*, willing her thoughts.

"She moved here to be best friends with me, of course." Kirsten laughed and as though Sarah had just snapped her fingers and made a wish, Kirsten breezily changed the subject by asking Harry if he wanted to play chess.

She hadn't even noticed the chessboard lying in front of them on the trunk, but yet, there it was. *Where did that come from?* She suspected it had something to do with Kirsten. *Maybe she is more than a healer?* Since she didn't know the first thing about chess, Sarah leaned back into the comfortable green polka-dotted cushion and curled up her legs, quietly sipping her latte and listening to the conversation between Harry and Kirsten. She was vaguely aware of Harry continuously sneaking peaks at her, and to be honest, she felt flattered by it. It had been a long time since she had felt even the slightest hint of desire without some ulterior motive. It was nice.

Even though it was obvious they knew each other, Kirsten was asking him about everything, it seemed, and Sarah was thankful. She was able to learn all kinds of things about Harry and realized Kirsten was saving her the time of having to do a background check of him on the Internet later. Social media was a girl's best friend – well, next to diamonds that is.

As it turned out, Harry was a very accomplished thirty-two-year-old. He had played hockey in high school and had been so good he'd gotten a college scholarship to Yale, where he studied business and eventually became an entrepreneur at the very young age of twenty-four years old. He'd started and owned the chain of upper east coast pubs called The Brew, including it's flagship location just down the street, very close to The Broom & Cup. He only sailed as a means of pleasure and entered competitions here of there, mostly to keep "his crew entertained", he stated. Sarah thought it more likely he wished for the entertainment. The Craft had been his father's boat and after his father had passed from cancer, Harry had not been able to part with the schooner. That had stung her eyes a little, knowing what it was like to lose a parent.

As she watched Kirsten swiftly beat Harry in a game of chess, she felt shame wash over herself. She had gone to college with big dreams and accomplished nothing. Harry had lost a parent and hadn't just run away. True, she had lost her whole family, but a loss was a loss right? She had only bought an expensive car because she didn't know what else to do with so much money. Sure she'd given some to various charities but even that didn't provide much relief or fulfillment. She had yet to accomplish anything.

And then what, on an impulse? She had just picked up and moved to Salem because a *feeling* had said to? Her feelings, guttural instincts her father had called them, were always right. She just wanted to know where they were leading her. *Maybe my path is here. It does feel right.* She knew she was soul searching. *Trust yourself more*, she thought.

Harry was impressive. He had accomplished so much in such a short amount of time. She wondered though, if maybe he wasn't as solidly built, as he seemed. Maybe sailing was his version of running away?

Just as the game was over, Kirsten gloating and flaunting her nimble win with a happy dance, Sarah felt a chill and lifted her gaze to notice a woman watching her from the window. Her chill increased. The lady had dark, chocolate-kissed skin but definitely wasn't from here. She thought maybe the woman was from somewhere in the Caribbean. But because of the way the woman was looking at her, Sarah could feel the goose flesh rippling all over her body. The woman looked at her like she was a ghost. It was frightening.

"Who is that lady outside? Staring at me?" Sarah asked Kirsten, trying to keep the alarm out of her voice.

"What lady?"

When Sarah looked again, the woman was gone.

CHAPTER FIVE

That morning in the coffee shop had freaked Sarah out. After she left Kirsten and Harry, she hopped in her Audi, towel under her bum, and drove towards the docks and then, on an instinct, turned left to go north and follow the Massachusetts coastline. The cobblestone bumped under her tires but Sarah barely noticed. *Who was she?* That question circled and encompassed her thoughts. *Who was that woman? Who is Kirsten and how does she know so much? Who am I? Why do I feel connected to this place?*

As the questions continued to churn in her mind over and over, she found they were all-consuming. Next thing she knew, the car was suddenly pulling over and she was parking her Audi on the side of the road. There, right in front of her bumper, was an old Inn. She took note of the 'For Sale' sign and her body practically jumped out of the car.

Strolling to the front door, she peered around. *Nobody is here*, she thought. The breeze blew up from the sea, twirling her long raven locks, and she could see Winter Island in the distance. The place felt mystical and romantic, and she again sensed a connection. She observed the bare garden, *I can fix that*, she thought. Turning, she knocked. No answer. She knocked again. Nothing. She placed her hand on the knob and with barely a touch, the door opened.

"Hello?"

Again, no answer.

It must be deserted already. With a deep, consoling breath, she stepped her tall laced-up brown boot through the entryway. The falling façade on the exterior had made her assume this charming storybook inn was in need of major repairs; but upon first glance of the glistening interior, she now doubted that. The dark mahogany hardwood floors creaked with every step, and she found the sound soothing. The dark blue walls and cream moldings were in fantastic shape, not even in need of painting, and the tin ceilings whispered of decadence. Nothing was out of place, broken or disheveled. It was as though the place had only been abandoned yesterday.

Turning into the first room, a parlor, she envisioned patrons sipping coffee and reading books from the nearby shelves that were stocked with all the classics. She could see children playing checkers in the corner and drawing outside the lines of coloring books. As she continued through a pocket doorway she found a dining hall and could see dinner parties and dancing, men with brandy and cigars, women with card games. She swore she could hear laughter. Smelling sage and thyme, she continued through another doorway and into a kitchen. It was small but functional, and there was something pulling at her thoughts more, something familiar, but she couldn't quite place it.

She turned and screamed!

"What are you doing in here?" a sinister man growled at her. Unlike the daydream in her mind's eye just then, this portly – tart - fellow was very real and anger flared across his chubby features.

Trying to steady her breath, she slapped a hand over her rapidly beating heart. "I'm so sorry. I knocked, several times! I saw the sale sign and I'm interested," she waved her hand around herself to indicate she was meaning she was interested in the property. She wasn't sure she had just spoken English though, since the words rushed out of her in such a flood of anxiety.

"Then call the realtor and see this place properly. Can't you *read*?"

Sheesh! He was really grumpy. She thought it a bit uncalled for.

"I will! Again, so sorry," she ambled backwards the way she came, "really sorry, very sorry."

Sarah was out the door and dashing to her car, still trying to steady her hasty heartbeats. She had had more than enough excitement and all-out strangeness for the day. *Talk about an adventure.*

CHAPTER SIX

Sarah was sitting on her balcony the next morning, all curled up in a blanket and thinking about the past day's peculiar events when she heard a knock at her door. Surprise colored her expression as she discovered Kirsten standing there in her hallway holding a Candlesticks tote bag. But then again, whom else would she be expecting in a town where she only knew two people?

"Hey doll, you left your books at the shop. I thought I'd bring them by." Her explanation was just so simply stated, so matter-of-fact.

Sarah stepped aside and motioned for Kirsten to come inside. "How'd you know where I live?"

"I saw your car outside. I know the building manager and asked which one was yours," again, she phrased her sentence so matter-of-factly. "I love your place, but don't you think you need some furniture?"

She fleetingly glanced around her living room and saw four bare walls staring back at them. Sarah laughed, "yes I do, I just don't know what I want yet."

"Well I say go with your gut, ya know? You don't have to sit on every couch in the land to find the right one! Or maybe you do?" Kirsten joked with her eyebrows and then giggled herself into pirouetting around in the space in a delicate manner, letting her beaded skirt sparkle in the sunlight. "Or you could just have a wicked dance party in here every night. That could be fun too. In fact, I know where we could get an atrociously glittery disco ball."

Just then Hanks shot across the floor and into the bedroom, letting out what sounded like a huff of a meow before he jumped up on her bed. "I guess he didn't like that idea very much," Sarah laughed. "Here let me take those books." She took them out of the tote and placed them on her breakfast bar. There was a third book included in the bag, smaller, with a black cover and gold intricate writing, and not one that she had purchased. "What's this?"

"Oh! Yeah, so I noticed you only purchased comprehensive histories of Salem, but everybody needs a book on just the witch trials. It's like, Salem law, ya know?" Kirsten had an all-knowing twinkle in her eye, like she knew something Sarah didn't. "It's my gift to you. Don't worry, it has lots of pictures."

Had she mentioned her need for photos? "Well thanks, I love it! Are you in a hurry? I just made some coffee and was sitting outside for a bit. Would you like to join?"

"Sure, you bet. Plus it's not like we could sit inside anyway," Kirsten laughed and fanned her hands out beside her. The only chairs in Sarah's condo were on the balcony.

As they sat and surveyed the bustling Salem Harbor, Kirsten pointed out specific boats that caught her eye. Her insight into the community really knew no bounds. She told Sarah how some ships were wannabe pirate-sailors who were searching for treasure ships that may have sunken in the bays around the area. Ironically a ship near those was an actual tourist-designed pirate ship with children playing and being entertained with tales from the sea. Other ships were in the trade business and unloading cargo; and those stories were far less amusing. One vessel not mentioned was The Craft and Kirsten seemed to skip over it intentionally, as though that tale wasn't hers to tell.

Sarah was entranced by the stories that Salem seemed to hold. She longed to unlock its mysteries and the inn floated into her mind.

"Kirsten, what do you know about the inn for sale, about ten miles north of here and on the water's edge?"

"That old place? It's been abandoned for years, and though many have tried to open it up as a bed and breakfast location, the perpetually grumpy man who owns it seems to refuse to let it go. Why do you ask?"

"After coffee yesterday, I went for a drive and came across it. There was a for sale sign and no one answered...well the door was unlocked and I wandered in."

"Isn't that breaking and entering?"

"I think that is what the grumpy man thought too when he found me out in the kitchen."

"Sarah! What'd you do?"

"I apologized, profusely, and left. He told me to contact a realtor if I wanted to see it. But I have to say...there was something almost intoxicating about the place. I think I might buy it."

"And do what with it?"

"Open it as an inn of course."

Kirsten looked a bit skeptical but shrugged her shoulders. "If grumpy ass does sell to you, I'd be happy to help you in the renovations. And also, we've got to get you some furniture. I know everybody in town and I'll get you a deal," she winked.

Sarah thought that Kirsten was a general wealth of information, which reminded her of something she hadn't had a chance to inquire about yesterday.

"The other day, in the shop, you said I wasn't new here. What did you mean?"

Kirsten froze for a moment - as if collecting her thoughts and sifting through the space in her mind - then set her half-drank coffee on the outdoor wicker coffee table and turned towards her. "Do you remember the cards you drew? Death and Judgment?"

"Yes."

"To cut what could be a long reading short, you're about to start a new life based on past events. The second card meant an awakening is coming. There's a life path that has yet to be chosen." She paused, and Sarah thought it was purely for dramatic affect. "I bought you the book on the witch trials because I want you to read it. I don't know what you'll find, but you're in Salem for a reason. I truly believe that Sarah. The cards never lie."

"Do you think I'm a reincarnated witch? Back for a purpose?" She shook her head, "I'm no witch Kirsten."

"No, I don't believe you are, though I do think there's something mystical about you. You seem to have a certain instinct about yourself."

Sarah couldn't agree more. Hadn't her father always told her to follow her gut?

Her new friend took a deep breath. "Where are your parents from?"

"From Georgia. They moved to Missouri for my father's job when I was two."

"And your grandparents?"

"Same – from Georgia. My whole family has lived there for several generations worth." Sarah could see Kirsten's clouded expression in her eyes, something wasn't adding up in her mind. She thought it best not to mention her adoption as it was a subject she felt she should keep off the table.

"Harry's family has lived in or around Salem his whole life."

Sarah had no idea why she was bringing up Harry or why her own lineage was important, but she didn't have the opportunity to ask because Kirsten rattled on quickly.

"I'm going to tell you something, Sarah. You won't find it in any of the history books you'll read on The

43

Salem Witch Trials, but I sense eventually you'll find it relevant, even if only for a moment."

"Okay," Sarah said warily. *She sure knows how to set up a tale.*

Kirsten took another deep breath and Sarah thought, just for a split second, her eyes cleared like clouds parting in the sky. "There were two main families that fought for power throughout most of the seventeenth century here in Salem. One family, the Porter family, was more into the business aspects of life. In today's world they would be considered entrepreneurs. The other family, the Putnam's, were farmers and owned the vast majority of the land."

"Okay. So it was the Farmer and the Suit. I thought it was the Parris girls who cried out claims of bewitchment?" Sarah knew just a little about the Salem Witch Trials. After all, she had read and seen The Crucible once upon a time. Her high school literature class had required it.

"Yes it was. The Putnam's brought in a Puritan Reverend and most people, at that time, took the Bible as part of the law. Well, actually, the Bible was the law. The only problem with *that* was that the Bible could, and still can, be interpreted thousands of ways." She paused to take a large gulp of coffee. "Reverend Parris wanted money though, and he only intensified the bitter rivalry between the two families after the Porter's managed to gain enough supporters to vote down a tax levy that would pay Parris's salary needs. The Putnam power had not gained enough support, and Parris had been counting on that. "

"So Parris wasn't getting paid, and soon enough accusations of witchcraft started out of his own household," Sarah deduced. "Well Hells Bells, I guess there's nothing like telling the community that they need a man of God around more than playing into their fears of Devil worship. That would certainly demand a need for him within the community. But wasn't his slave was named too?"

"Well, my theory is that his slave, Tituba, was named as a witch so nothing seemed suspicious. If the Reverend's own home was being afflicted, he could not possibly be behind the public outcry that ensued."

"Tituba?" The name had an odd familiarity about it.

"Yes. She was the first to confess and, for some reason, the townspeople let her go when nobody else was let off. She fled for her freedom, but in doing so, had to leave her home behind. History writes her as a fortuneteller.

"Okay... you lost me. Why do I need to know any of this?"

"Here's the part that won't be in those books." Kirsten pointed in thumb towards the breakfast bar inside, "Tituba cursed the people she felt responsible for making her leave her home and give up her identity. She cursed the Putnam and Porter families for all eternity."

"No," she said in disbelief. "Eternity? So she really was a witch?"

"Yes, and a very powerful one at that. Rumor of

45

the curse has always floated through Salem, to this day actually, and as the story goes, both lines of lineage are cursed to never know happiness; they are to always feel hollow and be burdened with ruin. It was man's pig-headed stubbornness and refusal to lay aside their differences that caused the mark on our town history. Neither a Porter nor a Putnam has ever called a truce between the two families. No new bond was ever born between, therefore, the descendents are still cursed to this day."

"Would these descendents even know if they were cursed? Would they even know a truce was needed?

"To be honest, I don't know if they even knew back then. Why wouldn't they have wanted to get rid of a curse? Especially during a time when witchcraft was so aptly forbidden? People thought the Devil was living upon those who were charged with what I would simply call a gift. They thought it was an affliction and practically treason."

"Well, pride is a man's number one fault. The Porter and the Putnam families must have really hated each other if they couldn't settle a truce."

"I still want you to read the book Sarah."

"Why?"

"Do you know who the last known descendent of the Porter family is?" Kirsten fixed her gaze on The Craft, the very much broken and weather-beaten ship. "It's Harry."

CHAPTER SEVEN

Harry had been scouring out the damage on The Craft since sunrise and he was relieved when Callen showed up around ten o'clock that morning to help. Although, he'd been so preoccupied with his thoughts it was a wonder he'd even noticed the extra help.

"Been here long old man?"

"Old man? I wasn't aware that thirty-two was so elderly mate."

"Normally it's not, but you aren't looking too sea worthy at the moment, *cappy*," Callen extravagantly annunciated the nickname.

"I gather you've been talking to Mat." Harry couldn't argue about his appearance though. He'd gotten no sleep the past couple of nights and he found he was incredibly sore still from their last battle on the waves of the Atlantic. His arms and legs were bruised being tossed out of a dead sleep when the storm came out of nowhere that night, and his back had rope burns from harnessing himself to the helm so he couldn't be tossed out to sea when trying to navigate through the rough waters.

"I didn't sleep much last night."

Callen grinned. "You were dreaming of that girl from the balcony huh? It's okay, I understand. We were at sea a *very* long time."

"I'm not *deprived* if that's what you're getting at pup. And the lady's name is Sarah." Harry could not deny that Sarah had been consuming his mind though. He'd thought about her constantly the last few days.

"Pup? I didn't realize twenty-eight was so young," Callen mocked. "And when did you meet this mysterious vixen? Go climb up that long black mane of hair and play prince to her princess?"

"Twenty-eight is young when you act like a kid. And her name is Sarah and, yes, I did meet her. It was outside Kirsten's shop actually when I, uh, accidentally made an ass of myself."

"Kirsten eh?" Callen's ears visible perked up like a puppy. "Did she ask about me? And of course you made an ass of yourself. I would expect nothing less."

Henry ignored him and continued the story, "I dumped my coffee into her car. A really *nice* car."

Callen hooted and hollered and rolled with laughter. "You.Are.Such.An.Idiot," he said in-between laughs. "You really have the worst luck man!"

It's called a curse. "It gets better. She drives a Audi R8 Spyder, and the convertible top was down."

"Holy witches! That's a nice car." Callen was salivating.

"Yeah, tell me about it. She saw me drop it while I was stuttering, drooling and making myself look as pathetic as damn near possible. If she hadn't said something, I don't know how long I would've stood there. Kirsten clearly took pity on me because she suggested going to get a replacement coffee. The girl was definitely trying to give me a leg to stand on."

"At The Broom & Cup I suspect. What happened next?"

"Nothing. Kirsten and I played chess, and she somehow got every single detail about my life out of me too. Sarah just listened - she didn't really talk much about herself, or even at all, now that I think about it.

"So now, she basically knows everything about you? And you know nothing about her?"

Well, she doesn't know I'm cursed, Harry thought. "Yeah, something like that."

Callen worked on removing a torn sail from the boom. "You know, you could just go and ask our favorite little witch about her. You and I both know that woman knows everything."

Harry grinned. "You just want to know if Kirsten likes you."

"Oh she does, she definitely likes me," he said with a lop-sided grin. "It's just getting her to agree to go out on a date with me that's the problem."

"Right," Harry mused. "Most girls reject dates from guys they like."

"Timing, mate, life's all about the right timing. And... it's just that...you know how she can read people? It's hard for me to ask her out and *not* think about what the end of the date could bring. I get wicked befuddled."

Harry shook his head. "Schmuck. If I were Kirsten, I would *always* turn you down too, you idiot. Can't you keep your thoughts PG long enough to ask her out?"

Callen groaned. "I try old man, I try. It's not like you're any better. You dumped coffee into an R8. And normally you're so smooth with the ladies," Callen teased.

"Smooth with the ladies? Who are you right now? Don Juan?"

Callen threw the torn sail into a bag and groaned. "Whatever bro, just go talk to Kirsten."

"Yeah, Mat mentioned the same thing this morning when I was grabbing breakfast. He said Kirsten always knows when something is right. Apparently she helped him and Ally get together way back when."

Mat and Ally had known each other most of their lives but had never even thought about dating until college when Kirsten hinted to the both of them that they should give a night out a whirl. Callen was right of course. Kirsten *was* funny like that and she really did know everything. *She should have a psychic shop, not a bookstore*, he mused.

Furthermore, Harry knew he liked Sarah from the first moment he had seen her on her balcony. Only he hated to admit it because of the curse. What if something happened to her because of him? Bad luck followed him like a storm cloud and he knew keeping a distance was be best if he wanted her to remain unharmed.

After all, it was all he could do to keep his businesses successful, which is why he owned them in name only. He had had to hire managers to run the pubs because he wanted to see them flourish and his curse would just bring the roof down. His father had warned and warned him against opening The Brew. He always told Harry that he was only asking for trouble.

Well, these days Harry *was* asking for trouble. He had it in his mind that he should be fighting the curse and when the storm approached so suddenly, he chose to steer The Craft right into the winds. It had been stupid of course. He'd put his whole crew at risk because he was bitter. Why should he have to live with a curse because his ancestors were narrow-minded fools? It hadn't been Harry that had made of enemy of the Putman family. No, it had been the Porters who'd been too narrow sighted to end their useless war. And they were the ones responsible for creating the mayhem that became The Trials, not Harry. He was tired of paying the price of the curse bestowed on the Porters.

Now here he was, glued to a town that was famous for being infamous. Somewhere deep within, though, Harry knew he was trying to sow the seeds of a deed only a devil would cherish.

But am I willing to bring Sarah into my curse, he thought. There was no denying that there was definitely a spark between the two. Harry wasn't a monk; he'd dated women over the years and had never felt anything. Not one of those women had ever struck him

51

dumbfounded – stealing his thoughts and breath all in one fair swoop. No, she was special. He wanted to know more about her. Callen was right about one thing that morning; he would have to visit Kirsten's shop.

"Callen, do you want me to ask Kirsten if she'd double date or something?"

"Wicked. Thanks old man." Callen grinned ear-to-ear.

CHAPTER EIGHT

Sarah sat on her bed contemplating between the two books she had bought and the one Kirsten had given her last week. She ultimately chose to open *Salem: A History* first. The only thing she knew about Salem is that the town was known for the 1692 Salem Witchcraft Trials. She wanted to know more about the town that had eventually embraced their tarnished past and developed a mammoth-sized tourism industry based off The Trials. The public schools, bars, shops, restaurants, museums, and boats… everything was named for witches or magic or something relatable.

People also said 'wicked' a lot. Every other word in the entire state of Massachusetts seemed to be wicked. When Kirsten and Harry played chess last week, every good move had been 'wicked great' and every ill move had been 'wicked bad' in its own right. Sarah wondered if people even realized how often they used the word.

Hanks jumped up on the bed and laid on top the book Kirsten had bought.

"We'll read it later buddy."

He meowed in response and rolled over, belly up. He was rather mouthy for a cat.

Sarah sighed and twisted her long dark hair into a bun so it was out of her face. Scratching his tummy with one hand, she opened the book she had already chosen with her other, and began looking through the pages.

Salem had been at the mouth of the Naumkeag River in 1626. Originally on a Native American site, the town was originally named for the river and modified to the name Salem three years later. A settler, Roger Conant, began a fishing company and started a trading center out of the village. It only survived two years before being taken over by John Endicott. Other areas like Marblehead, Peabody and most of the North Shore were originally part of the village as well. *Other towns that also have witchy legends*, she mused.

There was a photo of a document from 1639 for the first church of Salem. The only signature she could make out was from John Endicott, who by then had become the Governor's Assistant. *I wonder if the job tasks then are as they are now?* A few pages after the document she found another photo, this time of his death certificate. It stated the man died in 1679. Sarah assumed he must have been very important to the development of the town's history, but couldn't fathom why.

She flipped a few more pages and saw a drawing of two girls, Betty Parris and Abigail Williams – the two girls responsible for starting the witchcraft accusations. In the drawing they were playing with a Venus glass and an egg. A quick online search informed Sarah that a Venus glass was simply a glass of water with an egg white floating it. The egg white supposedly formed shapes for interpretation. It was a form of fortune telling – much like present concept of reading tealeaves The foot notes stated that Tituba, the witch Kirsten mentioned, was skilled in the art form and was the person responsible for teaching the girls how to read the shapes. Vainly, those girls used the Venus glass to seek their future social status and potential wealth by marriage, and would report these findings to other young girls in the area. Allegedly, on more than one occasion, the shape would reflect a coffin, a horrendous thought to those girls. *It was a sign. Hindsight really is 20/20.*

Sarah couldn't believe it. Naïve, silly girls had been looking into their future husbands, *even though they would've never had a say in their own marriage back then,* she disgustingly thought, and yet this somehow was demonic activity? It was out of that situation that the accusations of witchcraft began.

Betty Parris had started forgetting chores and appeared too preoccupied to pray. *Yes, she was probably too preoccupied, what, with daydreaming of a perfect husband and all*, Sarah thought, *seems more like a case of teenage hormones*. Then Betty would start throwing tantrums and say it was the Devil's affliction. Reverend Parris thought prayer would heal her, but Sarah could safely assume there was no such luck in that being a cure.

Sarah sighed as she reached for the book Hanks had vacated to go nap on top the fridge instead. It was the book Kirsten had brought over. She flipped through it, and then stopped when she glimpsed an eerily familiar face in a drawing of a woman named Tituba. *It couldn't be*, she thought. She went back to the other book and flipped until a drawing of Tituba popped in that book as well. Both of these pictures were original drawings from the trial journals, drawn by two different artist and yet, the woman looked identical in both drawings. The photos seemed identical to her memory of the woman who had been staring at her through the window of The Broom & Cup. *It's just not possible* she thought. *It's not.*

Convinced her mind was playing tricks on her, she pushed Kirsten's book back and pulled up *Salem: A History* once more and turned to the next chapter. During the War for Independence and the War of 1812, Salem had become a seaport for privateers. By 1790, Salem had grown to become the sixth largest city in the country, with the seaport known worldwide. The spellbound moment in time seemed all but forgotten by then.

Nathaniel Hawthorne, the author of 'The Scarlet Letter', had been born in Salem as well. He'd also written 'The House of Seven Gables', which most believed was influenced by a home in town. The community had since opened a museum in Salem in Hawthorne's honor. *Definitely checking that out*, she made a mental to-do note in her mind.

Prosperity had left the town adorned with Federal mansions and architectural delights. Sarah was floored by some of the beautiful homes that had been restored. A few of the houses were the original homes of judges during The Trials. Most of those homes had been made into museums at some point, while others are supposedly haunted and hosted tours, (as though a tour proved the theory of ghosts in some way). She flipped through the pages to see if she could find the inn mentioned anywhere to no avail. It was as if the building hadn't existed until she found it.

She skimmed through the book until she stopped

at somewhat-recent photos of Washington Square, which was an eight-acre plot in the center of town dedicated to the town of Salem's founder Roger Conant. The area was beautiful. Sarah thought it would be a lovely space to sketch in the Fall.

The next page caught and held Sarah's attention. She found photographs depicting Halloween over the decades, starting in the 1950s. Each photo, taken on October 31st at midnight, was of the "All Hallow's Eve Ball" the town of Salem hosted as a tradition in the Willows. The square had been decorated in lights, which became more intricately and skillfully woven through the trees, ball after ball. The night looked so romantic and dreamy with the soft lights adding to a glow already provided from the starry skies and the man in the moon. It was traditionally held every ten years, which meant there would be a ball this year. *What must a ball be like*, she wondered?

Sarah looked closer at the most recent photo to see if she recognized any faces and gasped. She did recognize a face all right! It was Tituba's, she was sure of it, and she was staring right at Sarah. She flipped to the previous page that and saw the same woman - the same age - was in that photo too, still staring at her.

She searched through each of the All Hallow's Eve Ball photographs as though it was a game of Where's Waldo. Tituba, or someone who looked *exactly* like her, was in each of the photos. Her hair or dress would change with the time period, but there was no denying that the face was the same as the face in the drawings from 1692. It was the same face that had been outside The Broom & Cup during the wicked chess game. *These photos have to be doctored – someone's idea of a sick joke.*

Sarah shut the book and Hanks leapt back on her bed and crawled into her lap. It was a comforting feeling and Sarah needed it. *It's just not possible. The same woman? Year after year?* Sarah felt so confused and so nauseous that she curled up on her bed and closed her eyes. *How was it possible unless Tituba was indeed...a real witch? And why is she staring at me?*

--

Sarah slept the rest of the afternoon and through the evening. She wished it had been a restful peace. Her usual dreams were filled with nightmares over the next few nights. She dreamt of the trials and of the silly nine-year-old girl Betty Parris seizing with afflictions. She dreamt of the Putnam family, head-to-toe dressed up in pilgrim-like outfits. They were all so plain in their appearance of mousy brown hair and dull brown eyes, no expressions. None of the women peeped a syllable and the men were constantly and exhaustingly laboring in the fields. All, except for one. He was sneaking off, running into the barn, and glancing over his shoulder before he entered and shut the door. He moved with a wide strong gait to the back of the smelly building and sat down on a small wooden stool in front of a lady with shadowed midnight hair. Sarah sensed an unusual connection with the stranger. She wore deep burgundy and blue colored clothing and gold decorated her fingers, bracelets woven around her wrist and a golden braid was wrapped around her neck and tucked into the bodice of her dress. In front of this woman set a mirrored glass. *The lady is a gypsy*, Sarah realized.

Wishing she could see the familiar woman's face, she started forward but her intuition told her to hesitate.

Sarah felt a chill and glanced around. *Was someone else there?* Her eyes turned upward to see Tituba standing on the straw loft above, staring down at the couple. Her eyes were lit with pure hatred and anger.

CHAPTER NINE

A few days later, when he could stretch his body without groaning, Harry stepped into Candlesticks with two hand crafted-coffee beverages as a tender. It could not hurt to offer a bribe before pouncing Kirsten for information. He was a gentleman, after all.

"Hey, Harry! I'll be right up!" A voice shouted from the basement below.

"How'd ya know it was me?"

"You smell like the sea and coffee. Who else would it be?"

Harry rolled his eyes. "Callen, maybe?"

Kirsten came through her stockroom door with a big box of glow stick wands, tarot cards and witch hats. She set them behind the counter. "Yeah, like he has the warlock balls to come into my shop. He mostly admires me from afar." She saw Harry eyeing the boxes she set on the floor. "They're for October. With the tourist season starting, I thought it best to start getting out the big sellers. People who have no idea how to interpret tarot cards just love to buy them anyway. Especially when they come from Salem. Oohohohho," She said in a spooky voice and twittered her fingers at him. "Oh, is that chai tea latte mine?"

Harry laughed, "Of course. I'm not going to drink it. OR drop it," he teased as he made a big show of placing it gently on the counter. "What's up Kirsten? How have you been?"

"Tired actually. I've been furniture shopping a lot lately."

"Why?"

"For Sarah's place, silly." She was so matter-of-fact, like Harry should've just known that answer. Often times, with all the knowledge and secrets floating around in her head, Kirsten forgot that she usually knew more than everybody else. "Her apartment was completely bare when I went to visit her. You know me, I saw bare, boring, plain white walls and an open space and thought *project*." She splashed her jazz hands up and did a small twirl.

"Are you letting her have a say at least?"

"Of course. I am not that controlling and I resent the insinuation."

"Oh," Harry put his hands up, "my bad. I must have been thinking about some other girl who decorated The Brew and also The Broom & Cup, on her own and without anyone else's opinion - *or* permission. What was I thinking?"

Kirsten grinned, "that I have phenomenal taste." She frowned, "Sarah's not really taking my advice though, except for some decorative accents here and there. She said she doesn't need to make a fashion statement, she just needs it to be *comfortable*," she grimaced.

"Oh Lord, the travesty, the horror." Harry had excellent mocking skills.

"Hey! Do you want me to help you with her or don't you?"

That sobered him up. "That obvious?"

"I think the whole town knows. And if not, at least everybody in The Broom & Cup does... and all the people who were outside Candlesticks to watch your *dashing* display of debonair. And of course, everybody in the Commons that day. Even Mat took notice of you staring at her repeatedly."

"Was I staring? Nah...nope, I don't think I was."

Kirsten leaned over her counter, smacked Harry on the back of the head, and then returned back to the other side again. "You were staring. Hard core. It was a gawk-fest. I mean she snuck peeks too, but you? You stared. HARD. You were practically slobbering on my poor bishop piece."

"Did not."

"Did too.

"Not."

"Guess you don't want my help." She jutted her chin out and dramatically sighed. She went about stocking her supplies and placed some witch hats on the counter for sorting.

Harry flinched. Dealing with a white witch, who supposedly had healing powers, could be a real hit on

63

your pride and self-esteem. "I want your help Kirsten."

She fluttered her chocolate eyes and tilted her curly head. "Say please."

He groaned. "Please help me." He felt emasculated, he really did.

Kirsten held her finger up for him to wait a minute, strolled back into her stock room and returned with an envelope. "I have four tickets left to sell for the All Hallow's Eve Ball. Two for you to buy and two for Callen to buy."

"A ball? That's your help?"

"Yep. Sarah would never admit it, but she's a romantic at heart."

"But I'm not."

"You are too, Harry. You just never had a reason to be until now. Try being a little romantic yourself. Trust me."

"So you're saying she's what? The Juliet to my Romeo?"

"Um no, they *died*. You're more the Mr. Darcy to her Elizabeth Bennett."

"*Who*?" He was lost.

"Pride & Prejudice is her favorite book. It's one of the only things she had in her apartment the first day I was there. Perhaps you should try reading it."

He groaned. "Would I be able to stomach the movie?"

"Possibly." Kirsten placed her empty coffee cup on the counter. No wonder she spoke so fast, she drank caffeine like it was nothing. She was a regular Gilmore Girl in the verbal speed category.

Harry paid for his two, very expensive, Halloween party tickets and put them in his wallet. "Can you tell me about her past?"

A twinkle flashed in Kirsten's eyes. He knew she was thinking that there was more than one type of past in her eyes. "No. I can't." At Harry's pathetic look she added, "she'll tell you if you ask."

Must she be so cryptic? He turned to leave but then he remembered Callen. "Hold the broom! You want Callen to buy the last two tickets? For whom?" She flushed and he lifted his eyebrows with an 'I knew it' expression. "You have a thing for Callen?"

"Oh shut up Ellison."

"Why won't you go on a date with him?"

"He's never actually asked."

"Wait - what do ya mean?" This stumped him. Callen was always talking about Kirsten. Harry just assumed the pup had asked her out.

"He starts, gets all nervous, stumbles around a few incoherent syllables and then… just abruptly exits the way he came. Every time he walks away and leaves me hanging. Every time," she aggravatingly emphasized. "I figure if he buys two tickets, one with my name already on it, it's a guaranteed date."

Harry chuckled. The pup was right, Kirsten did have a thing for him. He then laughed even harder at the idea of Callen being such a chicken. "Alright I'll tell him. Say, would you give me Sarah's address? I want to invite her to the ball today, while I still have my nerve."

"Sure, but you should take some tomato soup with you."

"Why?"

"She's been sick the last couple of days. A cold or something I guess."

"Really?"

"Yeah she fell in the water while she was checking out that old inn up near Winter's Island. The klutzy thing. She said she was walking through what will be a pumpkin patch garden, tripped, and splash! She fell into the cold Atlantic."

"She's interested in that old inn? Does she know the owner is a permanent jerk?"

"I think she's gotten the picture, but she's drawn to the place. I think she plans to make the old goat an offer and re-open the inn, after some extensive renovations. If he accepts it, that is."

Harry's curiosity was peaked. That old building definitely had character, but no sale had ever gone through. Rumor was the owner felt the inn would choose the buyer. Harry thought the guy probably just had seller's remorse.

"But at any rate, she did catch a chill. Take some soup with you if you're going. Something of the vegetarian variety."

CHAPTER TEN

Sarah felt like she could sleep for weeks with her stupid cold. *How had she even managed to trip like that?* She couldn't sleep though, because every time she closed her eyes she dreamt about the Putnam family, barns and Tituba.

No, instead, she was watching old movies and laying on her brand new cream-colored sofa underneath a black and pink quilt that Mat's wife Ally had given her as a welcome to town gift. Apparently she had taken up quilting when she'd gotten pregnant, like it was a craving or something.

Though she hadn't gotten much furniture yet, she'd made sure to get a huge overstuffed couch that screamed comfort, a coffee table – that was really a huge antique traveling trunk – and her then favorite piece which was an antique cabinet that she turned into an entertainment center. The cabinet, in fact, had been the only piece Kirsten truly approved of. That girl was decorating for her own house, not Sarah's. She laughed to herself at remembering Kirsten's face when Sarah had picked out a basic "boring" couch. Kirsten wanted her to get a bright red one that looked stiff, like a person wasn't allowed to actually sit on it. Didn't that defeat the purpose of a sofa?

Knocks at the door startled her, causing her to spring to her feet too quickly and have to fight off a wave of dizziness. When the sensation passed she shuffled in her slippers over to the door and peeked through the peephole. *Crap! What's Harry doing here? Kirsten. I'm going to kill her*.

"Just a minute!" She yelled, her voice sounding a bit coarse. She gathered all the tissues off the coffee table and ran around in a circle. "Trashcan, trashcan. Did I even buy one? Bathroom!"

She threw away the tissues and checked herself in the mirror. Her thick wavy hair was in a loose side-braid, *not too bad*. She had no color though. She pinched her cheeks and then winced, regretting it. *Ow. Why do they put that in movies? It hurts*.

She took a deep, albeit ragged, breath and swung the door open. There was Harry, charmingly strong with his ocean-blue eyes looking so cheerful, standing at her door with groceries, tissues, flowers and an umbrella for the rain that had been drizzling down all day. *Was he really this sweet?*

She stepped aside for him to enter her place. Goodness, the food smelled yummy. *Please don't be a dream* and her stomach growled in echo of that sentiment. Nothing was sexier than a 6'2 ginger-haired man bringing over a care package tucked into muscular biceps. Kirsten had been right about one feature – he did have a nice butt.

"Sorry to drop in on you, I didn't have your phone number. I was at Candlesticks and Kirsten told me you were sick. "So," he gestured to the tote bags, "I brought you some of the things that I like when I feel under the weather." He set the bags down on her counter and went about unloading the delicious aromas of food.

"You like flowers when you're sick?"

"Doesn't everybody," he said coyly. "No," he gently smiled. "I saw these and thought you may like them."

She took them from him and put them in an old champagne bottle that she had turned into a vase. "I love daises." The yellow of the blooms made her think of sunshine. "Thank you. Kirsten will be happy to know I've added some color to my décor."

He grinned. "Surely by now you've realized she considers her taste to be the best in all the land." He chuckled and returned to the other stuff he brought. "Ok, Kirsten also said you were a vegetarian so I brought tomato soup and grilled cheese sandwiches."

Did I tell Kirsten that?

"I didn't know if you still ate dairy so I brought both regular and dairy free options for the sandwiches." He laid out the food that had obviously come from a restaurant.

"Where in town do they make grilled cheese sandwiches with alternative dairy products?"

"My pub, The Brew."

Sarah was impressed. *SOLD*, she thought.

"I also brought tissues, orange juice, lots of cold medicine to get you drugged up and possibly put you in a coma, and a crossword puzzle book."

Sarah smiled. He'd bought her food and games to keep her busy. *Was she swooning?* "Did you bring enough for two people to eat?" He took out another bowl of soup and a sandwich all wrapped up with cauldron-printed paper. She laughed and he looked pleased with himself.

They set on her couch, she on one end with her feet propped up, and he on the other, eating and easily conversing and sharing stories; allowing the drizzling rain outside to cast a relaxing spell upon them. Her voice sounded strained but she hadn't smiled so much in such a long time that she would gladly take the pain.

"I can't believe you're watching this!"

"Marilyn Monroe is a legend, thankyouverymuch."

"I think its Jack Lemmon that makes the movie, personally."

"Not Tony Curtis?"

"I was never a Curtis man myself."

"What's your favorite Jack Lemmon movie?" *Please do not say Grumpier Old Men*.

Harry laughed, "Hmmm. Probably Alex and the Gypsy."

"Oh I love that one."

"You've seen it? I'm impressed Felix, not many people know it. It was my grandma's favorite, I used to watch it with her."

"That's so sweet. Oh wait, one of my favorite parts is coming up."

Sarah and Harry paused their conversation long enough to watch the part of the movie where Jack Lemmon's character comes back from his date as an engaged woman. The only problem was that he was a man! They laughed together as Jack Lemmon lay on the bed shaking maracas and singing about his love of being so admired by such a wealthy man. When he showed off his new engagement present, a diamond bracelet, to Tony Curtis's character, Sarah found herself fighting back the tears in her eyes.

"This was my grandfather's favorite movie." Sarah hadn't meant to share such a personal detail, but it just slipped out.

"What was he like?"

And with that, she felt her inner dam crack open a bit. "Gentle. He worked with his hands a lot." Had it been that long that she'd gone without speaking about her family? Sarah set down her bowl of soup on the coffee table. "He used his garage for a carpentry shop and would build rocking chairs and doll houses, things like that. When I was a little girl I would sit in the workshop with him. He'd give me a few nails, a small hammer and some spray paint." She smiled at the memory. "I would always end up hurting myself or painting his pants gold, but he'd smile and act as though I had just made a masterpiece." She paused for a moment, "and he always smelled like freshly split wood and cherry cough drops."

"Cherry cough drops?"

"Yes," she chuckled, "he kept them in his sock drawer and I would sneak one like it was candy every time I was at my grandparent's home."

"He sounds like a good grandpa."

"He was the best." She looked down, trying to hide the sadness in her eyes. "My whole family was great... they were the best."

Harry leaned forward and took her hand, feeling a warm spark from her tiny icy fingers as he did. "Can I ask what happened?"

Gosh, it hurt to recall the memories as she felt the words tumbling out of her mouth, "They died. They all died, my parents and my grandparents. I was twenty and in college." Her lungs were hollow and her heart ached.

"That's terrible. I am so sorry..."

"It's my fault," she said in a small voice. "They were flying to see me and the plane crashed." A small sob escaped her lips, her sapphire eyes wet. "They were the only people on the plane that died. Everybody else lived. *Everybody*. It was my fault," she repeated. "I swear, since then, living without them has been a curse." Sarah couldn't see the pained look in Harry's eyes, but as he hugged her, she could feel his sorrow.

It was as if the whole world had shifted when he took her into his arms. Outside lightning flared and the wind howled at her now rattling windows. What had seconds ago been a light, sprinkling shower turned into a roaring thunderstorm. Yet, she felt the calmest she had in years.

She had no idea how long they stayed there so powerfully glued together with an electric current, humming between them. This was a sensation that neither knew existed and that neither could truly describe. Why was it that every time they touched there was a literal spark? It was as if there was a thread weaving it's way from her heart to his, and their touch initiated the intricacy of the stitch. Sarah was aware, on some level, that she barely knew Harry. But, then again, she had somehow always known he could exist. And perhaps for the first time, she felt her soul stir awake inside her. It was an exhilarating and intimidating moment – almost unheard of.

When they finally broke apart, her tears now dried, the power had gone out from the surge of the storm. Sarah arose from the sofa and strode into her kitchen to dig out the candles Kirsten had made her buy, for which Sarah was now eternally grateful. Once the brightly glowing candles were lit, Sarah found herself curling up into his muscular frame, the electric current back, the thread weaving once more the moment they touched, and she told him her story. Adoption and all.

"I always knew, not that it wasn't obvious when I had black hair and everybody else was blonde. But my parents were my parents in every way. They adopted me when I was just a week old and I never knew otherwise. I loved them with all my heart."

Sarah sat there waiting for Harry to respond and when he didn't, she continued. "I feel so guilty inheriting their money and spending a dime of it but at the same time, it is what led me here, and to the inn I'm going to buy. I started to wonder about, you see, for the first time in my life, where I had come from. Who had given me up as a baby? All I knew is that I had to visit Boston, where the adoption agency was that my parents had used. But when I got there, it had burnt down just days earlier, no trace of my records were left. I was so angry! But then suddenly I look up, see a sign for Salem, and now here I am. New life and soon-to-be new career."

"You're really buying that old inn? Rumor says it's haunted."

"Rumor says this whole town is still full witchcraft."

"Point taken."

An awkward silence fell between them. She set up, breaking the humming current between the two. "Harry?"

"Yes."

"I know you're a Porter descendent."

He was obviously taken aback by the abrupt change in subject. "How...how do you know that?"

No point in denying the truth. "Kirsten."

"I never told her that. I've never told anybody."

Sarah shrugged. "I don't know how she does it but with her, you don't have to say a word. She just knows things."

He ran his hands through his hair and over his face, seemingly aging in an instant. "What is it you're asking me Sarah?"

"Will you tell me about the curse?"

"No."

"So you *do* believe in it. Why?"

"It doesn't concern you."

She blanched. "What if it does? What if I am a Putnam descendent?"

"No, you can't be."

Standing up, she ignored how dizzy she became, and teetered a pacing movement around her living room, deep in thought. "But think about it Harry, it makes sense. I was drawn to this town. Drawn like a magnet! And I have no idea of my origin. What if I'm the descendent? What if we're the one's who are supposed to break the curse?" She stopped pacing and talking with her hands to face him.

"It's just not possible."

"Why? Why isn't it possible? I was adopted, Harry. You don't know my heritage," she reiterated.

"Sarah, it's not possible," Harry said, raising his voice. "I've traced and traced the families, all the lineage. The last Putnam descendent died in 1918. He never married and he had no children. The line died out."

"How can you be sure?"

"Because I am."

"But-"

"Sarah, stop. I understand you want answers and to know about your past, but this isn't it."

She felt so defeated and slumped back down on the couch. "So you believe that you are just what? Cursed forever?"

"So it seems." More silence. "You are very accepting of a curse on a man you just met Sarah."

"I'm open-minded."

"Maybe you shouldn't be."

"Why?"

In my experience, curses don't bode well for the carrier. Would you really want that burden?"

Sarah sat back. She already carried a burden and she was sure it was heavier than anything he knew. The loss of her whole family devastated her – daily. She would never overcome the emptiness she felt every time she wanted to pick up a phone and call her mom for advice, only to remember she couldn't.

"Get out." She was suddenly choking on overwhelming grief and anger at her loss.

"What?" Harry questioned, confusion in his sea colored eyes.

She motioned outside. "The weather is letting up and I think you should leave."

Harry looked so baffled and Sarah watched the storm in his eye brew. "What did I do?" he asked, running his tanned hand through his bristled hair.

She strode to the door and opened it, "Some people have burdens they carry that are not of the mystical variety, but very real and very painful. Please leave."

Harry left, defeated and perplexed, as Sarah's tears rolled down her face. She didn't even bother trying to stop them. These teardrops were long overdue to fall.

CHAPTER ELEVEN

Harry flopped over in his bed, unable to sleep. He'd blown it not realizing what he said would push such a heavy emotional button for Sarah. He'd been talking about his own curse, Tituba's curse, not about the death of her family.

Even with a pit in his stomach from the day's events, he wished that Sarah could be right. It was astounding how much he wished for her to be right. If she were a Putnam then his curse would be over. To add insult to injury that day, not only had he been kicked out, but also a car had crashed into his truck while he'd been parked at her place and he had to walk himself home after watching his ride being towed away. The curse was definitely not over and it felt as though the universe had sent him a nice little reminder.

He tossed over again. Harry wanted her to be a Putnam. He wanted the excuse to be around her, to be with her. But would that be enough to end the curse?

In truth, it didn't matter because he just wanted her. He was furious for ending his romantic gesture the way he had. Harry had loved seeing her pale face light up with a smile at the yellow flowers. *How did I put my foot in my mouth so badly?* He should be pissed at Kirsten, too, for even telling Sarah about the Porter/Putnam curse, but he just couldn't. No he couldn't be pissed because now he would never have to explain himself. Kirsten had really done the heavy lifting for him, and had likely done a better job of it.

He was surprised Sarah hadn't mocked him, and at how easily she seemed to believe in the curse! *She believes in it because her family is dead and she's all alone*, he told himself. *She wants a reason for being alone. She doesn't want to feel guilty anymore.* Harry knew what that was like. He'd felt extreme guilt when his father passed away years ago. Harry hadn't been there because he'd been out at sea – sailing away from his responsibilities.

Before he was fully able to grasp his exhaustion, Harry was soon drifting into a nightmare. He stood in a cabin and before him was an unfamiliar site. The room was simple and he could make out a plain weathered table and some shabby chairs by a hearth that had flames spilling out of it. Before him, he watched as a man held an authoritative tone and took out his anger over some kid. *The Porter family*, he realized. John Porter, Jr. was nearly in a fisticuff with his own father, John Porter, Sr. Harry stepped closer to hear the argument and was surprised to learn it was about marriage.

Junior wanted to marry a Putnam girl and his father was telling him no. "It's forbidden," he said. "No son of mine would dare marry a Putnam girl and disgrace my family."

Smoke flooded his senses and the image before him faded into The Trials. Harry could see the Porter family, John Sr. looking much older, on one side of the hall and what he assumed was the Putnam family on the opposite side. John Porter, Jr. was there, not sitting with either family and appearing angry. He was staring at the center of the town hall and Harry followed his line of sight. The scene of this nightmare was audible before it became visible. The screaming and yelling was that of someone in agonizing pain. A young girl was writhing on the floor making unintelligible noises and pointing upwards to a woman who could only have been Tituba, Harry assumed, because her skin was much darker than the rest.

Then the scene shifted into a blur and Tituba turned to Harry. Everything stilled. The mist cleared around them and now only the two of them stood in the courtroom.

"She has her own magick." Then she smiled with a strange appearance of an all-knowing eerie gaze and the dream broke.

Harry woke up drenched in sweat. *What the Hell?*

--

Across town Sarah was stirring in her own bed. Once more her subconscious for forcing her to watch Thomas Putnam sneak into a barn and sit in front of the gypsy. *What a hypocrite*, Sarah thought.

Tonight she made an effort to ignore Tituba and walk herself around the table to sit next to the gypsy. Peering over the woman's shoulder and into the mirrored glass, she could see The Trials as a girl screamed out in agony. Had this gypsy predicted the death and the town's hysteria that was about to unfold? Had she known nineteen people would hang and one would be inexplicably crushed to death? *Barbaric*, she grimaced. Had Tituba known all along? From the next sentenced uttered, it was apparent that Thomas

Putnam had known and not done a thing to stop it.

"Dooriya," the man spoke, "will ye be harmed?"

The woman raised her head and shook it slightly. Sarah kept her eye on the reflective glass, no longer interested in seeing the gypsy's face, but what surfaced through the smoking mirror made her gasp. The image was shifting and transforming. It was The Craft, Harry's schooner, limping into port like on the day she had first seen him standing at the bow. The picture was nearly a mirror image to Sarah's memory the day she had met him. *What could this mean? Was this reading for Thomas Putnam or for the gypsy?*

As if the Dooriya knew she was there, the woman spoke, her voice floated through the air like a hoary wind in the night. "I will live on many a year, do not alarm thy heart love. Survival will be true for all my daughters to come henceforth."

Sarah's world swirled and Tituba was in her face, violently shocking her.

"She has her own magick."

Sarah sat straight up in her bed, saturated in beads of sweat. *What the Hell?*

CHAPTER TWELVE

Sarah walked along Pickering Wharf with two Starbucks coffees in her hand. She had nothing against Mat or his place in town, but she was a Starbucks junkie at heart and she had to get her fix in at least once a week. After the early morning meeting with the inspector at the inn, her inn, she needed the fix. Sarah needed a person to talk to and so she sent a text to Kirsten, asking if she was up for a walk on the wharf. She sat on a bench, under an aged maple tree, and waited, knowing her new friend would join her soon enough.

She placed the cups down on the bench and leaned forward to pick up a fallen maple leaf, the corners slightly tinted a reddish-orange shade. It was proof of the colder season rolling in, as though summer had never happened. She closed her eyes and thought of Harry and then released the leaf into the wind with the idea that it should land at his feet. *A girl can dream she had that gift*, she thought.

She regretted their argument and her involuntary reaction to something that should've been a simple conversation. With all her heart she wished she hadn't brought up her family – it had just made her so emotional and she wasn't ready for that.

Glancing up she saw Kirsten and her blonde curls bouncing up to the bench. Sarah picked up a chai latte and offered it to her. "I feel like I'm sneaking contraband," she laughed.

"Don't worry," Kirsten said, "that's how I feel every Wednesday morning when I skip The Broom & Cup and grab a cup of Seattle's finest instead." She grinned evilly and took a long sip. "One gets over the guilt after a few sips of heaven."

Sarah laughed. "It's our secret." Ceremoniously they tapped their cups together.

"So what's up?"

Sarah sighed. She had asked her friend to meet her because she wanted to talk about Harry's visit. It had been a week since she'd seen him, and even though he'd sent apology flowers, she felt unsettled.

"Well, for starters, I signed the papers at the inn. By Halloween, I will officially have some roots here in Salem."

"That's great! I can't believe that cantankerous old goat sold it to you! That man really has no charisma."

"Let's just say I made an offer that soothed his ruffled feathers." And man had she. She wanted the property so badly she had offered cash and above full asking price.

"That can't be all you wanted to talk about." Kirsten's perception was too sharp.

"Secondly I want to talk to you about Harry. He came to my apartment last week, no doubt thanks to you, and we had an *interesting* conversation."

"Yep," Kirsten said, not bashful at all. "I bet you did."

"You do?" Sarah was perplexed. *How could she possibly know?*

"He asked you to the ball right?"

Sarah, again, was puzzled. "No. He didn't. Was he supposed to?" The idea gave her flutters in all the right places. *A date with Harry*, she smiled inwardly.

"Oh." Kirsten frowned and Sarah had an inkling the girl was not used to getting her predictions wrong. " It's just that he bought the tickets from me and said he was going to ask you." Sarah visibly drooped. "Maybe he just decided to wait until closer to Halloween."

"But that's now only four weeks away."

Kirsten, too, looked confused as she scrunched her face up. "That's why, I guess, I thought he'd asked already. I was going to see if you wanted to go gown shopping with me? Now you probably don't want to."

"I'd love to, regardless of whether or not I'm going to the ball. Who are you going with?"

"Callen. He's Harry's first mate on The Craft." Kirsten's whole existence swelled with so much giddiness about her date that she was blushing like a sixteen-year-old going to her first prom.

"I've seen him, he's *really* handsome."

"Yes.He.Is! But I wonder what happened to Harry? May he just..."

"Forgot," Sarah interrupted. "He probably forgot."

"That's not like him."

"Well, it'd be understandable. Our conversation was kind of deep." *And weird. And emotional. And awkward.*

"Oh." Kirsten didn't ask for details and Sarah appreciated that trait.

Choosing to skip the bit about the fight, and the fact she had kicked Harry out, she continued, "Yeah, actually, that's really the reason I needed to talk to you. I was wondering...this is going to sound bizarre, I know, but...do you think it's possible that I'm a Putnam descendent? That maybe the curse shadows me as well? I feel drawn here, drawn to Harry. Ugh! I know how weird that just sounded! It's crazy!"

Kirsten leaned back into the seat of the bench with her blonde curls swishing over her shoulders, thinking and sipping her drink. Without looking at Sarah, she answered, "I wish I could say yes, but I honestly don't know." She turned to face Sarah, "And if anybody should know, it's me. My whole mind seems consumed with nothing but secrets, spells and tales."

It was Sarah's turn to slump into the bench now, radiating with disappointment and not even bothering to hide it. "I thought maybe you were psychic or something."

Kirsten chuckled. "No, no, I'm not psychic Sarah. I mean, fiddlesticks I wish I were! I'm just really, *really* good at reading people. Body posture, stances, facial and eye expressions, all these nonverbal signs tell me everything a person is thinking. I long ago perfected this "non-craft" as a way of selling more in my shop. I know, I know, it's terrible of me to do so, but it really flatters the tourists. Honestly, I'm not even aware of when I'm doing it anymore. I'm sorry, Sarah. I've probably been freaking you out a bit."

"I convinced myself you knew and could see things that I can't."

"Well, I *can* see auras."

"You can?"

"Yes. And you know what? Harry told me the first time he saw you, from the ship, you were surrounded by a pink light."

"Well there was a beautiful sunrise that morning. He was in a bit of that pink glow himself."

"Pink means Love, Sarah. It surrounds you even now."

Sarah set there, silent, for a few moments and then chose to ignore Kirsten's last statement. "I just thought that I was a descendent, I really did. I mean, when I came to Salem, just to visit, I felt this surge around me as though the actual place itself was telling me to *stay*. I guess you could say it was like a missing puzzle piece clicking into place. There was an energy racing through my veins. And today, when I signed my life to the inn, that energy raced even stronger."

"I admit, I felt that energy around you too, the first time we met." Sarah looked inquisitive again and Kirsten added, "And no, you are definitely not a witch.

But I had hoped, for Harry's sake at least, that you were a Putnam. But you're from Missouri and said your family was from Georgia. I just don't see it being a plausible theory."

"I'm adopted, actually, from a Boston adoption center. The day I drove into Salem I had actually gone to visit the center. But it was gone, destroyed in a fire just days earlier, leaving no method of tracing any information."

Kirsten froze for a second, looked over her shoulder and then hopped up from her seat, "Let's walk a bit, it's too cold to sit here in this wind."

Sarah really hadn't noticed a breeze but she stood anyway because she'd already learned that with Kirsten, there was usually a reason behind her oddities. A stroll down the wharf toward the dock restaurants wasn't going to hurt her.

"What did Harry think of your suggestion?"

"He told me it wasn't possible." Sarah peered out over the water and wondered how calm it really was beneath the surface. *Was it more like her*? "He said he had traced the lineage of both families and that the last Putnam descendent died in 1918."

"If Harry's says it's not possible, then it isn't. Nobody, and I mean nobody, wants that curse dead and gone more that him. He's turned over every rock in every possible path, I'm sure of it. I've always felt as though he thinks this place isn't even a home for him because he can't get comfortable. He was comfortable once upon a time, I think, but something would always go wrong. The first time he opened The Brew he thought the curse was silly and actually tried to manage it. It was not long before accidents began to occur on a frequency that was unnatural and, finally, he gave up his dream. He's since hired managers and rarely has he stepped foot inside since. Yet, he can't leave this town behind either."

"Ah, that's why he has The Craft, eh?" Sarah deduced. "It docks here but it sails freely with the wind." Her heart ached from him. Harry was inexplicably tied to Salem by the curse. *It must feel like time standing still for him.*

"Exactly." Kirsten glanced at her watch. "Hey, I hate to do this Sarah, but I have to get back to my shop. Are you going to be ok?"

"Yeah I'm fine. I just thought it wouldn't hurt to ask a witch," she smiled.

"You believe in me so easily, so judgment-free. The world could use more of you, Sarah Felix. Don't forget to call me when you get your invite to the ball, okay? I'm positive Harry will ask you." She started away and then turned back to Sarah with a wickedly beaming grin. "And do not, under any circumstance, let Callen know I can't read minds. It's far too much fun watching him squirm."

"Deal." Sarah watched Kirsten retreat in the direction she had arrived until she was out-of-sight. Something was a little more eccentric than normal in her behavior today.

She turned and walked south along the water,

consumed with the disappointed reflection of her wayward thoughts. She felt like somebody had crushed her with a stone the way the witch hunting villagers had crushed Giles Corey to death during The Trials. *May he rest in peace*, she thought. Drowning in her mind, she continued to walk until the clouds began to sprinkle and she turned back. *Where did everybody go?* Other people had been on the pier too that morning, she swore it, but now it was deserted.

When the drops picked up into heavy thick sheets of rain she brought herself to a halt. She couldn't see where she was going anymore and the docks were so slippery she was afraid she'd fall into the water. Should she wait it out or try to make it? And then, she felt it. An overwhelming sense of dread washed over her and ice raced up her veins, frosting her body over.

"I guarantee you've never felt the pain Giles Corey felt when he as *murdered*."

The voice was menacing and Sarah was sure she had stopped breathing. She moved her body around slowly until she came face-to-face with the woman who had been watching her outside The Broom & Cup that first day she met both Kirsten and Harry. It was the same woman she had seen in the photos, year-after-year. It was the woman haunting her dreams. "Tituba."

"I see someone's been doing her homework." The woman sneered at her.

"How? How is it possible you're here?"

The woman smiled. "I never left."

"But…how is it that no one's ever noticed?"

"People see what they want to see, Sarah. Mirrored glass ball or not."

The image of Dooriya flashed into Sarah's mind. "I'm not a gypsy Tituba."

"You think not?"

"I know I'm not."

She started circling Sarah, the rain not even touching her. "How have you been sleeping, Sarah? How's Tom Putnam been?" Her accent was laced with an accusatory tone.

"He's been a hypocrite; seeking his own future but damning others who do the same. It's you causing those dreams?"

"Are they bothering you?"

"N-no." She was starting to shiver with the cold rain reaching her bones.

"Liar." Tituba scoffed at her.

"Fine. They are bothering me," she yelled. "Why me? I'm not a Putnam."

"You don't know who you are, do you? Or what you are." Even through the heavy rain Tituba looked as ominous as she sounded. She was enraged and … evil.

"Who am I?"

"A gypsy for starters. And one who's trying to end

my curse. I want to know why?"

"Can I end your curse?"

"Whatever for? Harry? He seems resigned to it. And until you came into town, he was going to die alone and bury the curse. Isn't that the impression he gave you?"

"He hasn't done anything to deserve a curse. Why should he have to pay for his ancestor's stupidity?"

"What do you think I've been doing all these years *gypsy*," Tituba screamed at her. "I've been here to watch my revenge play out! My life was destroyed! Detonated from an epidemic called fear! If I had to pay for his ancestor's stupidity, so should he!"

"But why stay here? Why not leave like you were supposed to? This hatred will not bring you peace! It will not end your grief!"

"Don't you think I've tried to leave? I'm tied to my own curse! An unknown bond created by a gypsy who used her own magick to ensure that more than just the Putnam and Porter families suffered. She wanted me to suffer too! Don't you know that gypsy magick is different than a witch's magic? It can weave into the threads of connections without any living soul ever knowing. And now I'm living in a world that's made a mockery out of the Hell I lived through, laughing at my pain! Innocents and witches alike were executed simply for being *different*, for not being a Puritan. This town has been rejoicing in my village's horrid history! They have named the schools here after witches and damn near every shop in town! They're making money off death! Off *murder*. Those people were my friends! My neighbors! They have made celebrations and festivals and museums from it! And you ask how I could want revenge?"

"I ... I didn't think of it like that. But the townspeople aren't thrilled with such an ugly history either! It's not even about you!" Tituba was in her face in less than a second and it took all Sarah had not to scream off her lungs.

"Isn't it!" she screamed, and then repeated in an intimidating whisper, "Isn't it? I taught those foolish girls to read an egg in a glass of water and they believed it was really witchcraft. Betty Parris was the only girl to show any real promise. And she turned on me, didn't she? She couldn't handle being judged and seen as different. And she not only wielded the knife that stabbed me in the back, she twisted the blade repeatedly." Tituba backed off of Sarah. "Pity, I hear she went a bit crazy in the end," she smiled, truly showing her nasty side. "I don't think back stabbing worked out too well for her, the poor dear."

Sarah had to control the exchange. "Can I end the Porter-Putnam curse?"

"Only if you're meant to." It was barely an audible whisper but Tituba's statement was like a slap in her face.

Sarah blinked, confused by what she meant. And then, with a flash of lightning so brilliant it blinded, Tituba was gone and the downpour came to a standstill. She stood in frozen disbelief of what had just occurred. If she hadn't believed in sorcery before, she did now.

Suddenly Pickering Wharf was bustling with people again and not one other person had seemed to notice that the sky had just flat out dumped buckets of raindrops the size of Texas. They were walking around in dry clothes and there was not one puddle on the ground and yet, she was soaked to the bone.

By the time Sarah got home that afternoon she had visited two magick shops, picked up several books, candles, scents and crystals. The most important thing she'd bought was a crystal ball with a mirrored base. It was the closest thing she could find to resemble the glass from her dreams, and it was the first thing out of the box when she walked through her condo door. Immediately Sarah took it into her bedroom, Hanks underfoot, and slammed the door.

CHAPTER THIRTEEN

Harry could hardly contain his laughter as he ran into Kirsten and Callen picking out Callen's tuxedo for the ball. She was forcing him to try on cravats, cummerbunds and bow ties in every color of the rainbow. He followed her around like a little whipped pup and Harry was well beyond tempted to take a few photos with his cell phone and send them to his crew members. Callen, very masculine and a self-described ladies man, was *definitely* one sad little pup. Harry shook his head and walked towards the couple.

"Hey guys."

Kirsten, surprised to see him, jumped back from Callen as though she had been caught with her hand in the cauldron casting a spell. "Hey! What are you doing here?"

He gave a, 'seriously, you cannot be that daft' look. "I'm here to pick out a tux for the ball."

"Oh yeah, you finally asked Sarah?"

"What do you mean? I asked her last week, when she was sick." *When we got into a gnarly fight that I don't even understand.*

"Uh no you didn't. I just had coffee with her yesterday and when I asked if she was excited about it, she said you hadn't asked her." She pranced over and slapped him on the back of the head, "why haven't you asked her! I gave you a foolproof plan! Did you forget?"

"No!" He rubbed his head. "I thought she would've seen the ticket by now. I put it inside one of the crossword puzzle book I gave her. I even wrote an uncharacteristically sweet message with it!"

"Dude," Callen said, "did you invite someone on a date via a bookmark?"

Harry reddened. "I thought she would find it cute, I left a little note in the book for her to solve puzzle thirteen. Now she probably thinks she's not invited. Damn it." The shop owner raised a brow and Harry's cheeks went from cherry to plum. "I'm an idiot," he chastised himself and in a quieter voice, "This is your fault, Kirsten. You are the one who told me to be *romantic*," using air quotes around the final words.

"Do not blame me, Harry." Her eyes took a glazed appearance for a moment, "And do me a favor - don't call her to tell her where the ticket is. Leave it to Fate. Trust me." Her face cleared back to her mischievous normality, "Also, next time, let's discuss the ideas you think are *romantic*, okay?" she mocked his air quotes.

"Kirsten, I can't just leave this to Fate. I want to have a date and I would like for it to be Sarah. There's no point in going to that stupid thing otherwise."

She put a hand up. "Uh, the ball is not stupid. It's tradition. And if you and Sarah are meant to be, it will happen."

"What?"

"What's meant to pass, shall. I believe that Harry. And so should you."

"Yeah," Callen said, seeming annoyingly confident all of the sudden. "Besides, what's an All Hallow's Eve Ball without a little magic?" He swung his arm around Kirsten and the sleeves of the tux he was trying on ripped at the seam.

Kirsten smirked with a cat-ate-the-canary smile. How did she always manage to keep that twinkle of mystery in her eyes?

--

Harry could not *believe* he agreed to leave it to Fate. What an enormous chump of a loser he was going to be when he got stood up on Halloween. He wanted to second-guess his decision, he really did. But it was just that whenever Kirsten told somebody to do something, generally, they listened. The girl could rule the world if she wanted to. Harry didn't want to go against the curve, especially when he already had a curse looming over his whole existence.

He sighed as he stepped into The Broom & Cup and plopped down on a barstool, head in his hands, elbows on the cool walnut wood. He felt exhausted and it was no wonder, not sleeping well and all. He'd experienced more dreams about the Porter family every night for the last week. Harry could not make heads or tails of any of the images either, the scenes flashing like a movie reel in his mind. Why, after so many years, was he just now starting to dream of his ancestors? *Although everything feels more like a memory than a dream when I see it all happening in front of me.* It didn't make sense and honestly, he wasn't sure he wanted it to. His mind felt like a blur of information and he was feeling the onset of being freaked out a bit. It took a lot to shock a man out who resided amongst a town of witchcraft, magic and *curses*.

Mat set a steaming oversize mug of the blackest brew in front of him, the smell intoxicating his senses. "You look like you need the strong stuff today friend."

Harry lazily looked up at Mat, "that I do. Got any whiskey?"

"Nope. What's up?"

"I'm just not sleeping well."

"Dreaming about Sarah?" Mat quipped. "She comes in here almost daily now, you know, in case you haven't noticed all of her artwork that's taken over my back wall." Mat gestured with his hand toward the back of the shop. "She definitely has some skill. And, she's befriended Ally, so I advise you not to break her heart. My wife will have your head if you do." Though Mat was very protective of his wife, Ally could more than hold her own. Harry respected the pair, their admiration of each other, and protectiveness over their friends. He considered them family and would never knowingly disappoint them.

"Well I'm having some nightmares of late, but they have nothing to do with Sarah, mate." He sighed, took a huge drink of coffee and burnt his tongue. *Figures.* "In fact, I have no idea what they're about." *Not totally true but no reason to burden Mat.*

"If you ask me, I think you're just dreading the next seven months or so of being land-locked. That's a long time for you, cappy."

"Ugh, yeah, you're probably right man. Bloody winter," he grumbled.

"You could always migrate south for the winter, with the birds. Everybody around here will sure miss your wonderfully chipper moods though."

"Smart ass."

Mat chuckled. "Hey, I have to get it all out here. Ally's forbidden my sarcasm at home until my son is born."

"It's a boy? Congrats man, that's awesome! Feel free to name him Harry. Or Tucker. I'm not picky on how you name him after me, just that you do."

"Thanks, I'm pretty excited about it having a mini-Mat. And if he's being named after anybody, it's me. You know," he slowly continued, "Sarah's offered to help out here once he's born, that way I can spend more time with Ally and the bambino. Well, when she isn't busy with the inn of hers of course. That's quite the project she is aiming to undertake."

Sarah was going to help out at the coffee shop? Maybe it was just him but everybody in the town seemed to be falling for that girl. "That is nice of her."

"Yeah it is."

"She's really serious about that old inn? Nobody's operated it for decades."

"She swears it's been amazingly maintained inside."

Harry had his doubts. It was a well-known fact around town that the irritable fellow who owned the property was a hermit. And Harry just couldn't picture him being a handyman. "It means she's willing to put down roots in Salem though."

"As long as you don't break her heart."

"Why do you think I'd break her heart?"

"I mean, being a guy, it beats me. But according to Ally, every girl you've ever dated has ended up with a broken heart. I told her that two to three dates maximum shouldn't leave a girl in shambles, but she swears man. Every girl, every time."

"That's ridiculous."

Mat nodded his head in agreement. "I told her it was more likely that Sarah would break your heart. People won't quit asking me about her. It's only a matter of time before she'll actually go out with one of these loons around here."

"Thanks man, you really didn't have to tell me that." *And I'm the idiot who agreed to leave his future with her to "Fate". You're a moron Harry Ellison.*

Harry swirled his head around to survey the coffee nook and could see the artwork Mat had mentioned. He stood up and winded his way through the mismatched-but-matching furniture to have a better view at the drawings. *The Craft*, he mused. She *could* see his ship from her balcony, just as he had seen her. She was amazingly talented - the lines of his ship had been executed to an astounding likeness. Every curve, every groove was there. In the next piece, she had captured the storm that he weathered the night before he first met her, before he could have even fathomed Sarah, or even envisioned a world where a woman like her existed. The image of the storm was so accurate to what his experience had been, so life like. *Did she draw this from her imagination?* He still wasn't certain if it had been sheer luck or his carefully practiced skill that had gotten The Craft to safety that night.

The third portrait was of his ship in port, damaged but repairable, with a beautiful rosy horizon in the background, portraying the majestic sunrise, and Harry standing at the bow. To him, it was a portrait of where their story began.

CHAPTER FOURTEEN

Sarah had been staring into her crystal ball for two weeks and the only thing reflecting back was her face. Well not herself, exactly, but a woman who was very similar in resemblance to her. It was the gypsy from her dreams, Dooriya. She didn't see a Putnam or a Porter once. Or even Tituba. Just the woman who had eerily familiar features that included midnight black wavy hair and slightly different azure blue eyes that were tinged with violet. She noticed, though, that Dooriya's eyes would turn into more of a silvery shade when she was reading her own reflective glass.

It frustrated Sarah that she was obviously related to this gypsy somehow. But why was this so important to Tituba? What could it really mean? Tituba stated that the gypsy had tied her to the curse, which meant once the curse was broken, Tituba would be gone. *And then she won't be haunting my every thought, every dream*...Sarah wouldn't be looking over her shoulder every time she left her condo. If the Putnam family had truly died out, the curse would've died out too wouldn't it have? The only place she felt peace and seemed to forget these thoughts at all was at the inn, *her* inn. She had visited the property once more with an inspector and an architect to assess the needs of renovations, and found herself once again drawn to the kitchen. It was the only portion of the inn that was original and, though plastered over, the original log cabin walls were still insulating the room.

But Sarah was determined to find a remaining

Putnam descendent. She had even gone to the Boston library to research the ancestry of the family when she was supposed to be on a shopping trip with Kirsten. As far as she could unearth, Harry was right. The lineage appeared to have died out. Every dead end just irritated her more, to the point of wanting to chuck her crystal ball right into a brick wall.

She switched from her new obsession to her old one, and picked up her sketchpad. As she sat cross-legged on her bed, with Hanks providing a soothingly soft snore next to her, she sketched what consumed her thoughts. She drew Tituba, she depicted the barn scene, she charcoaled Thomas Putnam, and when she began to use colored pencils on an image of Betty Parris - she froze. Intently focusing her sapphire eyes on the face she herself had begun to portray, she gasped as her light brightened with realization. The Betty Parris of her nightmares looked quite a bit like Kirsten. In fact, in the way that she mirrored the gypsy in the barn, Kirsten resembled Betty Parris. As in, a relation: an ancestor. *Why haven't I seen this sooner?*

Sarah threw her sketches into a folder and stuffed them in her bag. Grabbing her car keys, she practically launched her Audi to Candlesticks like a broomstick flying through the stars, her wild raven mane fluttering in the wind. She recalled Tituba saying that Betty Parris had been the only one of those silly girls with any real powers. Was Kirsten really Betty? Was she still around like Tituba was?

Through her research of Betty Parris, Sarah discovered that Betty had eventually moved away from Salem and married in 1710. Her foolish obsessions and preoccupied wants of a husband at nine-years-old (in her homemade chicken guts of a crystal ball) had come true. Sarah hadn't thought to trace Betty's lineage. Why bother? She'd bet The Craft that Harry hadn't done so either.

She perfectly parallel parked her Audi precisely in front of Kirsten's shop and as she strode through its entryway, she flipped the OPEN signage to CLOSED. Kirsten was perched on her glass counter top, blonde hair cascading down to her waist, appearing as though she'd been expecting her imminent arrival.

"You know, this is the height of tourist season and that Halloween's next week? My store shouldn't be closed in the middle of the day. It's highly unprofitable to be putting up the shutters right now." Kirsten tilted her blonde head and curiously blinked, waiting for Sarah to commence.

Sarah looked around and couldn't locate a single patron in the shop. Outside there were adults, children and tourists alike walking around in witch hats and pumpkin-shaped shopping bags. Booths were set up all over the Salem Commons with trinkets and face painting areas. Funny though, not a thing was being displayed in front of Kirsten's shop, which had left a parking spot wide open for her.

"I don't see anybody in here, I think you're fine." She may have been a little snappy but Kirsten wasn't fazed.

"So what's up?"

"Did you know I was a descendent of a gypsy?"

"I had a feeling. I told you I sensed an energy around you."

"Really? Did you sense it? Or did you know my ancestor, Dooriya, personally?" Sarah thought the girl tried to look skeptical, but she wasn't that great at it.

"What do you mean? How could I have known your ancestor? That's an impossibility Sarah."

"Well perhaps more improbable than impossible. After all, Tituba certainly seemed to know Dooriya somehow. Or is she out of the question too?" Her large sapphire eyes widened with the need to know the answers.

Kirsten flinched a bit at the name. "Tituba huh? Let me guess, she visited your subconscious mind?"

"More like live and in person. And she wasn't in a great mood."

Kirsten hopped off the counter, looking unnerved for the first time since they had met. "She approached you?"

Sarah stood frozen in her disbelief over Kirsten response. "I don't get the impression you're shocked at what I'm saying."

"Because I'm not. She's never approached me, but I've always known she was here. I have sensed her presence before, many times."

Sarah fished her sketch of Betty Parris out of her bag and held it up so Kirsten could see. "Anything else you want to tell me?"

"I think you're artistry needs work, you got my hair color wrong."

"Oh this sketch isn't of you Kirsten, it's of Betty Parris." When Kirsten's face went white, Sarah knew the girl hadn't been lying about not being able to read minds, because if she could have, she would have known that the image of Betty was coming out. "So is she an ancestor? Or are you really she? Betty Parris? In the flesh? Are you just like Tituba and still here? Is that how you knew about Harry's curse?"

"That's a lot of questions." Kirsten swallowed hard. "I'm a Parris descendent, though, I'd prefer you not tell people that."

"Why ever not? It's not like you hide being a witch?"

"No I don't. And no witch should have to. But people are still, to this very day, not exactly thrilled with the nine-year-old girl who turned the community upside down and into a mass of paranoia. The world still fears others who are different. And a witch hunt by any other name is still a witch hunt."

"I agree with you. But if you aren't back from the past to haunt the future, how'd you know about the curse?"

"It was in my Book of Shadows. Most of the town secrets are. But I'm *not* like Tituba," she emphasized, "I'm not tied to Salem *or* to the curse she laid lifetimes ago."

"Then why are you here?"

"I like it here."

"Why didn't you tell me? Why keep everything so secretive."

"Tell you what, exactly? That you are a gypsy? You wouldn't have believed me because you weren't ready to hear it. I couldn't exactly provide proof either. Honestly, some things are best to discover on our own. If I had told you that Tituba was stilling roaming our fair cobblestone streets, you would've tried to commit me to a psychiatric ward. You may be extremely open-minded Sarah, but even I know there are limits. And I didn't tell you that I'm related to the Parris family because I'm not proud of their behavior. Who would be? You're now the only other person that knows, besides Tituba, and she's not exactly my biggest fan either." Kirsten's face showed very clearly that sleep often evaded her as well.

"You could've told me. At least about Betty Parris. I wouldn't have judged...you should've told me." Sarah had calmed her inner fears down, no longing choking on her heightened emotions.

"Well I'm telling you now, aren't I? It is only *now* that you have reached a place of acceptance. And since you're so Hell bent on knowing everything, you should know that I am not able help break the curse. Only Tituba or a Porter-Putnam bond can break it."

"I'll find a way."

"I don't doubt you'll try."

Sarah paused and tilted her head in the curious

manner Kirsten liked to use. "Next week's Halloween, and that creates a possibility that I don't think Tituba has even considered."

Kirsten nodded as realization dawned in her eyes. "I hadn't thought of it either."

"I may need your help."

"Of course! Anything!" Kirsten beamed, "We are still friends right?"

"We are … as long as you stop hiding things about me."

"I'm sorry. I really am."

Sarah felt any remaining tension leave her body the way a balloon deflated. "Consider it all an after thought. We need to find out precisely where the Putnam land was. I need to go to a certain location – a barn actually."

Kirsten smiled. "I already know where that is." She moved over to a heavy looking Celtic chest behind her glassed shop counter and raised the lid off. She took an old, heavily bound, leather book out. "The old town map of Salem Village is in my Book of Shadows. This book has been passed through every generation since Betty."

Together the two of them, hunched over the old heavy book, searched through pages upon pages of the kept knowledge of the Parris generations, or at least the page numbers Kirsten would allow. Some, she said, were secrets that didn't need to be brought into the light. A thrill of victory shivered down Sarah's spine as they discover that the land, and the barn location of her visions, was still erect. It had remained undisturbed after all these centuries. A witch's magic, she was learning, could do incredible things to secure the threads of time.

Sarah was going to set Harry free and she was pretty sure she could do so with some aid from a few spirits. *Hopefully friendly spirits*, her thoughts chimed. Old folklore suggested that on Halloween, spirits could roam the Earth with other living souls. If there were no living Putnam descendents today, that didn't mean a past spirit couldn't help break the curse, right?

"Kirsten, I know it's tourist season, but come to the inn with me. I have a feeling."

"You're getting really adept at hearing your intuition speak to you."

When Sarah pulled her car up to the inn, with Winter's Island off in the distance, she saw an enchanting abode, a story waiting to be written. Kirsten saw a dump – it was written all over her face.

She laughed, "It just needs some TLC, but you'll be amazed by the conditions inside. I promise." She started up the stone staircase, her tall black laced up boots making small tap sounds under her heels. She fished a key out of her purse and twisted it into the old iron lock until she heard a click, and pushed the heavy wooden door open.

"Wow – I've never been in here. I don't know anybody who has. It's beautiful!"

From the entryway of the foyer, the inn's enchantment still spoke to Sarah. The dark wooden floors and carefully carved moldings, the pocket doors and the grand staircase – it made her fantasize of a life with more mysterious meaning, and all it's questions waiting to be asked. And it was hers.

"You should throw a masquerade here Sarah, on next year's Hallow's Eve. How wonderfully alluring and charming it could be!" Kirsten was swimming her thoughts in Sarah's own pool of daydreams for the place.

"Come with me to the kitchen, it's towards the back of the inn. I've felt lured to this specific room since I first stepped my toes inside this place."

Kirsten cooed as they went through each room and Sarah could see that the lust of the place was winning her over. She oohed and awed, letting her face glowed with astonishment. "I never knew any of this existed. It's wonderful."

As they entered the kitchen, Kirsten halted and gasped again, this time sharply.

"Kirsten – what? What's wrong?"

Kirsten gaped at her. "Your aura, it's changed. It's yellow. And royal blue but outlined in silver. I've never seen anything like it. It's beautiful," she whispered in awe.

"What does it mean?"

"Something inside you awakens in the room. Something spiritual. It's enlightening and I think you feel it to…the awareness I mean."

Now it was Sarah's turn to gape. She *had* experienced it, many times. "But what is drawing me here? And why only to this room?"

Kirsten chewed over the questions and then reached out her hand. "I have an idea. Take my hand and then concentrate on the magnetism you feel. The magnetism that is calling to your spirit."

Sarah did as she was asked and saw words slightly fall over Kirsten's lips. *A spell,* she realized. Though Kirsten always acknowledged she was a witch, Sarah had never seen her in action.

"You aren't concentrating."

Sarah looked sheepish and then closed her eyes. *Concentrate, concentrate…* she cleared her thoughts and then felt it. She felt the tug. She sought deeper and found the tug came from just under her breastbone.

"Sarah, open your eyes." Kirsten gently nudged her.

Again, she did as she was asked and she saw silver. No, a mist. *No it is silver,* she realized. A silvery mist had wrapped around her. *My aura,* she gasped. It was beautiful. The filmy fog twirled around her, as though it danced with her spiritual awakening. She gazed at it, watching as it twisted and transformed into a braid – no

- more like a chain, and thread itself out between her and the back right corner of the kitchen, to the wall.

"Follow it." Kirsten instructed.

Not letting go of her hand, for fear the connection would break, Sarah traced the chain to the wall it had secured itself to and reached out with her free hand to fan the wall where the chain was, and the spot pulsed under her palm. "There's something behind this wall."

Knowing she had found her answer, she let go of Kirsten's palm and looked around her surroundings, seeking out any blunt object she could find. "Aha!" There, on a high kitchen shelf adjacent to them, was a candlestick.

She popped up and practically ran across the kitchen tiles. As she began to climb on top of the counter, Kirsten tugged on her arm.

"Exactly *what* are you doing?"

It dawned on Sarah she hadn't explained her mad behavior. "I want that silver candlestick. I'm going to bust through the plaster."

"Get down, Sarah."

"But," Sarah looked down and saw the candlestick in Kirsten's hand. "Show off," she mumbled.

She returned to the corner the chain had linked itself to and took a big baseball bat type of swing. The plaster was old enough that it started to crumble upon the first swing. She kept repeating the motion until the hole was big enough that she was able to remove chunks of the wall with her hands. Through the surrendering façade she found the log cabin barrier from the original structure. It was incredibly aged and Sarah wondered how it could be sound after so many years.

She fanned her palm over the wall once more, and then, on an inkling, strummed her fingers into the grooves. As she found what felt like edging, she pulled but the wood was warped from time. Yanking once more, using every muscle she could manage, a piece of the wall – a hidden compartment – wrenched out of the wooden wall like a stuck desk drawer.

Kirsten kneeled down next to her, "Look!" she exclaimed in an excited whisper. "Does this make us pirates? Finding hidden treasure?"

"Sounds good to me. Although we might be the first-known gypsy pirate and witch pirate in history." Sarah retrieved a box from the interior of the original structure. It was strangely stunning and very heavy in her palms as she studied it. Vines of silver and sapphire wove into one another, wrapping around the cube of onyx. Opening it, she discovered a gold chain, twisted into a delicate plait, with the same intricately woven detail wrapped around a sapphire stone. She had seen it in her visions.

There, in her hand, was Dooriya's talisman. In her heart, she smiled as a missing puzzle piece to her existence slid into place.

"Out of curiosity, what are you going to name this place?"
"Spellbound. It'll be named The Spellbound Inn."

CHAPTER FIFTEEN

The night before Halloween was the worst night of sleep Harry had ever had, worse than sailing through rough waters even. Instead of the reoccurring dream of the Porter family that had haunted his sleep during the past month, he was standing behind a tree on the edge of a corn field watching as Sarah was ran through the harvested stalks towards a barn. She stopped, ensuring herself that she was indeed alone by hurriedly glancing around, and then proceeded into the barn.

Harry rushed out of the trees to follow her and came to a halt just shy of entering the barn himself. His ocean blue eyes widened as he heard voices, though he didn't recognize their owners. He peeked his head inside and saw the back of a man, dressed in the same pilgrimage garb he'd been seeing on a nightly occurrence since he'd met Sarah, sitting across from a woman whose head was down.

He took note of Sarah now, sitting beside the woman, and when he made the motion to move closer her head snapped up and she placed one finger to her lips, motioning for him to remain silent. He stepped closer, more quietly this time, and saw that the woman was fixated on a mirrored glass. *A gypsy*? No gypsy had ever been mentioned in any of the town's folklore. He peered over the man's head, but he couldn't see anything other than silvery smoke inside the orb.

It was then that the woman looked up at the man sitting opposite from her and Harry realized how much

117

she bore a striking resemblance to Sarah. Her face was more round, her skin a darker and sun-kissed, and her eye color was slightly different. It was not a sapphire-blue like the woman he knew, but she was obviously a relation of some sort.

Sarah must have already come to this decision because she was peering into the ornament in the same manner that the woman had just been. Harry still couldn't see a thing but Sarah must've been able to. She looked at Harry, then, her eyes seeming somewhat hopeful. She stood and walked around the table, took his hand, letting their spark ignite once more, and dragged him back a few steps as the scene around them whirled. *How is she doing this?*

In the mist of the confusion, Harry glanced up to see Tituba watching them. *She doesn't look pleased...* Was he in Sarah's dream? Had she been having the same type of memory nightmares as he? He did not doubt that anything he'd seen in his sleep lately wasn't real. These were all things that had actually happened in the past, during the time of The Trials. The two of them had stepped into bits of history. *But how?*

Sarah plucked him out of his trance by whispering, "This is new. This I haven't seen before."

So she was aware of him in this dream sequence. He wondered again if she was the person controlling it. Having been cursed all his life, nothing fazed or surprised him anymore when it came to the mystical balance of order.

Before him, now, Harry saw that the barn had faded into the night. In front of him stood the strange gypsy with a small bundle in her arms.

Sarah became conscious of the fact that when Harry had crossed into her dreams, he had obviously been having as many restless nights as her. And at this instant, holding his hand, she felt stronger. *Together, they were stronger*, she realized. Instinctively she had taken his palm into her own, and her intuition had been correct.

Presently standing in front of the two of them was Dooriya, with a small infant in her arms. She had never seen this in a vision before, but maybe it had been because Harry hadn't been with her. Maybe they were only meant to see this once they were together.

As soon as she'd figured out that these dreams weren't nightmares, but rather visions of memories past, she eagerly anticipated them every night. These were pieces of a puzzle, their puzzle, and allowing her to discover who she was – where she came from. Deep down, she knew Salem was truly a part of her. Reaching up she fingered the sapphire amulet she'd worn to bed. A sixth sense told her that her talents of perception and intuition had strengthened with the acceptance of what she now considered a gift. Never would she remove the charm from her neck.

She peeked towards Harry, still holding his hand, and allowed herself to feel the current between their two palms growing stronger, brighter. *It's the bond*, it dawned on her. Looking around, she did not recognize where they were. Dooriya was standing in a small, one room cabin, and Sarah could make out the gushing sounds of a stream nearby.

She then focused her attention and tugged Harry towards to Dooriya, careful not to let go of his hand. Dooriya did not notice them. No, not when the cloaked infant wholly consumed her in her arms. It was a teeny tiny little girl with angelic black curls and huge blue eyes. She crept closer and took note of a small pendant around the girl's neck. The gold chain was too long and it had been looped her throat, several times it appeared. The adornment was a cross with a small circle attached at the bottom. Inside the circle was a small rosette. Sarah had seen it somewhere before but she couldn't recall where.

Tituba wasn't in this vision. No, she was gone. Had this been after The Trials? Was she already in hiding? Or had it been before? Sarah had no idea.

She found herself unsure of why this memory-revelation could be important. If Tituba wasn't here, then she wasn't the one responsible for them seeing it now. She looked at Harry and watched as he stared at Dooriya. She guessed he'd figured out the relation because he appeared enthralled.

The scene around them revolved once more in a whirlwind and Sarah had to wipe the hair out of her face with her free hand so she could see where they were.

Hand-in-hand, they were standing by the water's edge as Dooriya placed her baby in a basket full of blankets, her own head hooded in dull fabric so nobody would know she was a gypsy. The baby girl, still festooned with the pendant around her throat, was

120

gently handed to an older couple on a small boat.

When Dooriya shed a tear Sarah realized she was giving her baby away. She obviously loved her child, so why would she do that? Sarah felt a deep sadness – she wanted to stop it.

Harry saw Sarah's reaction and whispered in her ear, "she's saving her. Unwed and a single mother wouldn't have bode well for her child. Not in that day. In a way, she's giving her daughter life. A rebirth."

Sarah studied his face and then looked at Dooriya, who was now gazing at her. The boat and the water were gone, and the three of them now standing alone in a grassy knoll under a blanket of stars. *Were they in Willow's Park?*

"I show you this," the woman said, "so you understand."

"Understand what Dooriya?"

"I am overjoyed with fulfillment that my sight shown truth. You did come, my daughter's daughter. Of my blood you are born and of my magick you know truths."

"Dooriya, what is it I am to know?"

"Your past is your present my dear."

Those words brought to mind a memory of when she was in Kirsten's shop and she had pulled the Death card. *You are about to go through major changes, some abrupt and some due to past events.* Kirsten's words swam though her mind and Sarah realized she had been spot on. *Well I'll be damned.* The answers had always been right in front of her.

And like the magick of a gypsy, Dooriya was gone, disappearing into the starry night with the visions in tow. Only the two of them remained standing under the moonlight in Willow's Park.

"Goodnight Harry." She leaned on her tiptoes and ever so gently placed her lips upon his cheek, feeling yet again the spark of their connection; slipped her hand away from the fold of his and let the scene blacken into the darkness of her now fully decorated bedroom.

Climbing out of bed, rustling Hanks awake in the process, she turned on her lamp and grabbed the crossword puzzle Harry had given her when she was sick. She needed something to keep her mind busy because there was no way she was going to be able to drift back into a peaceful slumber.

CHAPTER SIXTEEN

It was the pounding on her door that woke Sarah up that next day. It was the kind of knock that could wake the dead. As she trudged a path to the door, slippers muffling her steps, she glanced at a clock and was shocked to see it was already two o'clock in the afternoon. *Crap. I slept all day.* It wasn't a surprise, really, considering that she hadn't been able to go back to sleep until she had completed nearly every crossword puzzle in the book.

Not surprisingly, Kirsten was the noise-making culprit. Instantaneously, as the door opened, the girl whizzed past Sarah like a witch on her broomstick, both arms full of bags and fluffy dresses.

"Did you oversleep? I thought we were going to the Putnam's old barn this morning? Don't forget the ball is tonight, you said you'd help me with my hair. Where's your coffee pot? By the look of you, we're going to require two pots of your absolute blackest brew."

Dizzily, Sarah wondered if the twirling twister, created by Mother Nature herself, could have possibly fit any more words into that same breath and sluggishly pointed to her counter top where her machine was. "Espresso. Lots. Please don't put any eye of newt in it," she mumbled as she moved to sit at the breakfast bar. "And we don't have to go to the barn anymore. Nor do we have to find any roaming spirits today."

"Ha ha ha… so *funny* you are. No barn or spirits? Why not?"

"The gypsy had a baby."

"And this is important because…wait, with who?"

"I'm not su-," Sarah stopped as realization dawned on her and gob-smacked her in the face. Leaping up from the barstool, she rushed over to the antique trunk coffee table to retrieve the book Kirsten gave her as a welcome gift when she first moved to Salem. She plopped it on the counter, flipping through the pages until she came to the picture she was searching for. Hurriedly, she grabbed her sketchbook next and opened it to the picture in her mind's eye. *Aha!*

"What has you so distracted?"

"Kirsten, I'm a Putnam."

Kirsten sighed in frustration. "I thought we went over this. You can't be."

"No I am. I've connected it now. It's so simple, I can't believe I didn't see it sooner."

Kirsten placed a bowl-like mug of espresso with soymilk in front of her. "What are you babbling about?"

"Look at this photo! Do you see that pendant?"

"Yeah, it's an old Puritan symbol. There are five total. I've seen them on the memorial for those who died during The Trials."

"Look at who the man is wearing it!"

"Oh. Oh my wicked flying broomsticks! Wait- what?"

"I couldn't remember where I had seen it and then I remembered I had *drawn* it! Weeks ago!" She thrust her sketch at Kirsten, almost knocking her mug off the counter. "Last night I saw the baby wearing it!"

"You saw? Baby? What?" Perplexities must be new for Kirsten.

"Yes, in a vision that came as a dream. Harry was there too."

"And...baby?" She again questioned.

"The gypsy, my ancestor Dooriya, had a baby and kept it a secret. She had to give the baby up to protect the child, and herself, I think. But, before she gave the little girl away, Dooriya placed *this* pendant on her."

"Ah, wicked," she said as she excitedly clapped her hand, making her blonde curls bounce. "Do you think Harry has derived the same conclusion?"

"I guess it's possible, but I doubt he would have noticed or recognized this necklace. *Or* what it meant."

Kirsten walked over to the chair and picked up the garment bag she had carried in with every thing else she appeared to own. "Well then, my dear, we have a ball to get ready for. And I *still* really don't like that couch!"

CHAPTER SEVENTEEN

The ball officially started at eight o'clock that Halloween evening and it was now over an hour later, and Sarah had yet to arrive in Willow's Park. *Leave it to Fate, Harry.* He just may never listen to Kirsten's advice again. He felt like a complete idiot standing there alone, waiting. And it wasn't as though offers hadn't come his way in that long hour. Apparently Harry Ellison's tall, strong, muscular sailor frame in a tuxedo was a rare commodity. Even little blue-haired grandmothers were asking him to dance, which simply delighted his buddy Mat.

"She'll come, stop fretting," Ally said. Mat and Ally had arrived at the same moment as Harry and, like the great friends they were, stood by with him while he waited for an arrival that may never come.

"Have I told you how beautiful you look tonight, Ally? Green really is your color." Harry wasn't lying. Ally was marvelous in her emerald gown with her chocolate hair twisted into an up-do and her hazel eyes shining with glee and pure joy. She had finally entered her second trimester and she was positively glowing with happiness.

"You flatter me more than my own husband," Ally said with a wink.

"Hey! I'm standing right here!" Mat attempted to look annoyed, but he wasn't able to keep a grin off his face long enough to do so. He leaned over and kissed Ally's cheek. "You are always gorgeous, my dear."

Harry was grateful for the relief of the chuckle that escaped his throat. It really did ease some of his tensions. After that dream – or whatever it was – with Sarah last night, he wasn't sure what to make out of life anymore. *How is it that they could be so aware of one another? And walk in the same dream?*

It was obvious, now, that Sarah did have lineage here in Salem, but why would that even matter? The gypsy hadn't been a Putnam so her heritage wasn't going to affect the curse. And why did the dream end the absolute second she let go of his hand? He touched his cheek were she had caressed it with her soft lips, and was positive he could still feel the warmth from where their skin had connected.

"Hey, there's Kirsten and Callen! Oh my gosh! She's gorgeous! I've never seen her in so much color before but violet really works for her." Ally excitedly pointed towards the entrance where Kirsten and Callen were seen getting out of a familiar black Audi.

Harry's remaining high hopes plummeted as he realized Sarah couldn't be with them because that car - the very one he had dumped his latte into the morning he first saw Sarah up close and drooled like a puppy - that car only held two people. Surely Sarah would have come with Kirsten. Those two had been immediate best friends the moment they'd met. He watched as the newly formed couple posed for a photo op, Callen grinning from ear-to-ear, and then as they paved a pathway toward him, Mat and Ally.

"Why are you in such a sour mood?" Kirsten quipped.

"Gee, let me think: *Leave it to Fate, Harry. Trust me*," he mimicked.

Callen held up his hand to stop him. "Night's not over mate." He twirled Kirsten and whispered, "Let's dance babe," in her ear.

Harry thought they resembled teenagers with their apparent giddiness over being together. When he turned to make a comment to Mat about it, Harry almost spoke out to the thin, crisp October air. Mat was leading his wife to the dance area as well, leaving Harry to stand alone and watch the ball as a spectator. Crossing his arms he huffed to his lonely self. Turning, as he was about to leave and give up altogether, he froze as he heard...*hooves*?

Across the street, on the opposite side of where he stood in the square, a horse drawn carriage pulled up with Sarah holding center stage as she sat inside it. The whole square – the trees, the grounds, the tables, her carriage – had been laced with white twinkling lights. Harry thought that everything about the ball added an enchanting glow to her. The twinkle lights surrounded her completely, making her appear absolutely magical from where he stood, rooted in awe. *Was he drooling?*

In her small delicate hands, she held a gold candle in front of her chest as she stepped out of the carriage. Gracefully she made her way towards him and Harry was grateful the ground was there to hold him up. He had never seen anything more beautiful, she was angelic.

Harry swore every head in a ten-mile radius turned to look at the princess who had just entered the ball.

She wore a gold beaded, champagne-toned gown that snuggled her tightly in the waist and flared out into a full skirt from her hips. The sweetheart neckline showed off a sapphire stone dangling from her throat on a gold chain. The dress bared her shoulders but gave her sleeves that just covered her arms past her elbows. Her raven hair was pulled back with soft waves cascading down her back - it made her bright sapphire eyes stand out more than he had thought possible. Sarah was truly breathtaking.

Harry was still staring, and yes probably drooling, when Sarah Elizabelle Felix finally reached him. It had seemed to take her forever and yet - come what may - the moment had not been long enough.

She placed the gleaming gold candle on the table next to Harry and fished out a tiny scrap piece of paper from her clutch. The paper had been folded into a petite square and when she unfolded it, Harry realized it was a crossword puzzle. It was the puzzle he'd written his invite in the blank spaces instead of the correct puzzle answers. It read:

Meet Me Under The Stars on All Hallow's Eve?

"I'm not sure if you realize this," she said with an impish twinkle in her sapphire eyes, "but this is where we were standing last night, with Dooriya. Right here in this square, in this very spot, under these same stars."

He looked up at the night sky. "Now that you mention it, that night star on the left does look a bit familiar." He smiled with relief and found that it was mixed with an ecstatic joy, and he felt his nerves relax. "I'm so glad you came."

"I wouldn't have missed our first date for the world."

It was their first date, he realized. Hanging out with Kirsten or bringing her soup when she was sick definitely didn't count as dates. "It's funny, you know, that this is officially our first date because I feel like I've known you my whole life."

"I think we were meant to be, you and I. And not just because of our curse."

Our curse? "What do you mean? I'm the only cursed one here. It dangerous to even be standing near me."

She shook her head and smiled at him. "The Porter family is just has stubborn as us Putnam's, aren't they?"

Us Putnam's? "Sarah, we've gone over this. You cannot be a Putnam."

"Don't you remember our dream last night?"

"Who could forget it?"

"I thought maybe that you hadn't realized it."

"Realized what?"

"Whom the baby belonged to."

"It was the gypsy's child, there was no doubt about that."

She softly laughed. "Every child has a father Harry."

"Well, yes, I know that."

Sarah planted the paper inside her clutch and set the purse down on the table too. "Here, let me show you what I mean," she said. "Close your eyes." Placing her fingertips on each of his temples, she took a deep breath to steady herself, as the familiar electric current began to run through their bodies as their skin touched.

Harry saw a scene in his mind's eye. It was as though he was floating above a stage and watching a show from the rafters. Again he was in the Putnam's barn, but this time he watched as Dooriya came through the door, quickly followed by a man moments later. It was Thomas Putnam, Jr.

This scene was different though, because there wasn't a table and a reflective glass in sight. No, the exact moment the door closed, the Putnam son was kissing Dooriya! And she was fully participating back in the beginning of what appeared to be a tryst.

The setting altered to an argument between to the twosome, Dooriya's hands placed protectively over her belly. She was leaving him! The gypsy had no home and nowhere to go. Dooriya's family had disowned her for straying and not marrying one of their own kind. Thomas Putnam's family would disown him if they discovered that he had impregnated a gypsy...*a gypsy who looked quite familiar.*

It hit Harry like a punch to the face. Sarah had been right all along. She'd sensed it and Harry had not wanted to hear it. *Sarah was a Putnam.*

He heard a sigh and felt Sarah pull her hands back, letting the trance break. "You see," she whispered, barely audible, "we were naïve to think that the only descendents born were children from marriages."

When he finally opened his eyes and saw hers, they were widened with the acknowledgement of the truth. "Tituba wouldn't have known that when she laid that curse at our doorstep that a child had already been born." Harry felt an odd mix of emotions run through him.

"No, I don't think she did. She did know about Thomas Putnam's friendship with the gypsy though. Tituba thought it was the gypsy who had tied her to her own curse, but with magick." Sarah offered a small shrug and an equally small smile.

"It would serve her right."

"She is tied to it, Harry. She isn't set free until we are set free. And I know I would personally like her to be free and leave me alone."

Harry nodded in agreement and led her to the dance floor –ignoring the little blue-hair grandmothers faces of disappointment - and when he embraced Sarah, their electric current ignited again. "I love that feeling, by the way, every time we touch."

"Me too," she grinned.

"So, we don't hate each other like our ancestors and yet, the curse hasn't been lifted."

"How can you be so sure?"

"This is the second tux I've worn today. The first one met an unfortunate accident when I put it on."

"What's that?"

"It ripped at every seam." He laughed as her giggle erupted into a joyous laughter.

"I have an idea of how to set an end to our curse." She was blushing a little.

"Oh really? Is this idea painfully?"

"Only if you're a biter."

As she wrapped her arms around his neck, Harry barely noticed the wind quicken around him. Pulling his head down, his face to hers, Sarah touched his lips with her own. Harry felt her melt into his embrace and tightened his arms around her narrow waist. The fall foliage swirled into the air, arching and circling the couple as they embraced, light overtaking them. The spark of their electric current erupted into the sky like a shooting star and exploded into silver fireworks.

She leaned back, breathlessly, but stayed in his embrace. Sarah's sapphire eyes had tiny little silver flecks and her smile reeked of untainted happiness.

"I'm not sure if it's lifted. We better try it again," he joked.

Sarah leaned in for the assist when something moved in her peripheral view. "Look!"

To their left, at the entrance of the All Hallow's Eve Ball, stood the three faint figures of John Porter, Jr.,

Dooriya and Thomas Putnam, Jr. In Dooriya's arms was their baby girl. The gypsy smiled at them and, with a nod, the couple turned and faded off in the distance, reunited at last.

The bigger shock, to Harry at least, was Tituba emerging out of the crowd - that unknowingly parted like the sea - and after giving Sarah a curious glance, she turned to follow Dooriya and Thomas, with John falling into step next to her. With a breeze blowing through Sarah's raven hair, the twosome disappeared into the night. Spirits had indeed walked the Earth that night and Tituba's curse was finally lifted.

"Now," Harry said, "where were we?"

CONCLUSION

Though I came to Salem on nothing more than what I had entertained as a mere whim, it took less than two months for me to fully understand why I felt as though I had found my home - my familiar. To put it simply, I did. To discover that I had gypsy blood, and magick, running through my veins was an added bonus. And, as it turned out, my crystal ball had been with me all along in the form of my sketchpad.

The inn I had found myself magnetically drawn to was originally where Dooriya had given birth to a Putnam child. The log cabin walls I found in the kitchen were one and the same of the place where my legacy was born. It was, and is, my ancestral home now. By the next October season, The Spellbound Inn will house gypsy magick once more.

On that starlit night of the All Hallow's Eve Ball, the black curse lifted and a new spell - a spell of love - had been the bond to break it. I'm aware now that, while I had thought everything happened by chance when I moved to Salem, it was actually my intuition leading me to my Fate.

The Judgment card I drew at Kirsten's shop had said there would be an awakening: a rebirth.

As it turns out, that's exactly what happened. Dooriya's well-kept secret had set Harry and I free. Together, we feel as though we could accomplish anything we set our minds to. And my own gift, a gift of sight, has come into the light through this discovery.

The history books will never reflect the curse of the Putnam or the Porter families, the pages will never acknowledge Thomas Putnam's secret daughter and none will ever mention or know of my ancestor, Dooriya. I'm okay with this, though, because as long as there's someone who believes, then someone will always listen to the truth and as sure I am writing this, Kirsten will probably be the *one to tell the story.*

Though there are more stories to be written, and more mysteries to be unraveled, I feel as though this may be the appropriate place to end my tale. At least for now.

After all, some things are best left to the magick of our own imagination.

Sarah Felix (Putnam) Ellison

This Tale's End.

Aura's – What colors can mean

Red – Red aligns itself to the most powerful of colors and often is a fleeting color. The element attached to the color can be either positive or negative, as it can reference anger, lust, passion or even heart-related conditions as red also represents blood.

Pink – This color is often indicative of love and that of a sensual person. Pink can also indicate the owner of the aura as an artist or psychic. Dark pink, however, can mean dishonesty and immaturity.

Yellow – This color often indicates a playful nature, as well as inspiration and spiritual awakenings. A paler shade of yellow often indicates a repurposed sense of exhilaration or a spiritual ability discovered later in life; perhaps found on a spiritual journey of discovery.

Orange - People with orange auras can be the life of the party, but are also likely to be consumed by mood swings. Often scientific minds or those that have perfectionism needs carry an orange aura as well, as this color indicates a love for details and challenges in the mind and body.

Purple – Purple hues can be associated with those that daydream often. Often this aura reflects a compassionate and calm individual. Violet hues represent visionaries and indigo tones may show a seeker that can peer in-between worlds.

Blue – Blue can often represent a calm mannerism in moments of strife or crisis; clairvoyance and a deep sense of intuition.

Silver – Silver is supremely positive and often represents spiritual abundance.

Green – Green often reflects on those that find themselves to be healers, teachers or a natural communicator. A dark green could represent a jealous nature though.

White – White, often associated with angels, represents purity.

ACKNOWLEDGMENTS

First, I want to thank my parents for their unconditional love and support. You are amazing people; parents, grandparents and friends, and I strive daily to make you proud. Mom, thank you for the feedback on the story.

To my favorite sister-in-law Katie: thank you for being my editor. And favorite SIL. I look forward to working on more books with you!

To Mat Jennings: all other book cover designers should bow down to you sir. Thank you for your friendship and design talents.

To Padfoot: I think you are amazingly talented and I love the inspiration you bring onto those you come into contact with throughout this journey called life. I wish you all the best and more. Thank you for exciting and encouraging me to finish this story.

To all the #BAOB and #CREATURES I have met in life: thank you for giving me an outlet to continue my creativity all these years. I think it is YOU who has inspired me.

To any person living in Boonville, MO: I hope you have found the magic that continues to live inside Thespian Hall. It inspires me still.

AND, to all my friends and family who deal with my weirdness on the daily: thanks for never committing me. Seriously, I appreciate you.

LIZ RAU

ABOUT THE AUTHOR

Missouri born and raised, Liz Rau now resides in Denver, Colorado. As an avid and passionate supporter of the performance arts community, Liz's background & hobbies include dance, choreography, theatre and writing.

With a Bachelor of Science degree in Mass Communications from Southeast Missouri State University, Liz continues her education in communications while currently employed in the sales field; and actively travels throughout the world to the places that inspire her.

With six nieces & nephews, she often considers her role as an "Auntie" as one her greatest pleasures in life. She also dotes on her two cats, one of which is black & fluffy…perhaps the real-life inspiration for Hanks?

And lastly, to the concept of Fate versus Coincidence, Liz would like her readers to know she began writing this story in 2010. While creating The Trials: Secrets, Spells and Tales - Liz kept all storylines & character names to herself, including the use of the name Elizabelle. In 2016, Liz's fourth niece was born & given the same name (Liz is *not* a nickname for Elizabelle).

Fate? Coincidence? That's your decision.

LIZ RAU

Follow Liz Rau on social media!

Twitter – @LizRauOfficial

Instagram – @LizRauOfficial

Official Book Hashtag - #TheTrialsSST

Contact the author - LizRauInfo@gmail.com